I0618160

ROZ MACLAREN

Evernight Teen ®

www.evernightteen.com

Copyright© 2025

Roz MacLaren

ISBN: 978-0-3695-1178-2

Cover Artist: Jay Aheer

Editor: Jesterbell Editorial

ROZ MACLAREN

To everyone who's ever felt like they didn't belong.

ROZ MACLAREN

JANUARY

Roz MacLaren

Copyright © 2025

Prologue

Fourteen years ago

She could kill him.

The thought had briefly flitted across her mind before, when he first mentioned his plan for the twelve babies, but she had stuffed it down and buried it. After all, Ted knew what he was doing. That's what she'd always told herself. But now, with her fists clenched, and her heart pounding, *now* she really wanted to end this man's life.

The only light in the laboratory came from the director's office. He sat back in his chair, feet on the desk, while the young woman stood in front of him. Tears were shining in her eyes.

The man was smirking. "I put you in charge of this project because I thought you would do a good job as leader. Don't tell me my faith in you was misplaced."

The woman glared back at him. How had she ever thought this man was someone to look up to? Her voice shook with anger. "You lied to me, Ted. You looked me in the eye and you lied to me."

Ted shrugged. "I bent the truth a little."

"When I think about what the parents of those babies went through … what *you* put them through!" Jennifer looked down the floor, trying to blink the tears away. "And I helped you! I thought we were doing the right thing here!"

Ted jumped to his feet and came towards her. She took an involuntary step back, acutely aware of the height difference, of the fact that this man suddenly seemed transformed from friendly to threatening in the space of a second. "We are doing the right thing," he snapped. "Years from now, they'll revere us as heroes. We'll be the people who changed the scientific world as we know it!" He clasped her hands, and his grip was clammy and cold. "We're doing something revolutionary, Jen. Unfortunately, that comes at a price." He let her hands go, as quickly as he'd taken them, and his face changed. A darkness came over his eyes. "The question is, are you willing to pay the price? Or do I need to let you go?"

A lump rose in Jennifer's throat, making every breath a struggle. The hairs on the back of her neck rose as Ted went back to his desk and opened the drawers. He took out a gun as casually as if it were a pen and meticulously cleaned it. "Well, Jen?" He looked up at her with a snakelike smile. "Are you with me? Or against me?"

Jennifer couldn't keep the tension out of her voice when she said, "I'm with you, of course I'm with you."

Ted's smile widened. "Good. Glad to hear it. Now get back down to the lab and do your job. We've already lost five specimens. I'm not keen to lose any more."

"Of course, sir."

"And, Jen?"

"Yes, sir?"

"Next time you have any moral quandaries, keep them to yourself. Science is no place for the fainthearted." He flashed her a wide grin and replaced the gun in his desk.

Jennifer walked out of his office, closing the door as loudly as she dared to. She wished she was brave enough to slam it. Her heart was pounding, pulses beating in her fingertips. When she got back to her lab, her tears fell properly.

Seven babies lay in cots, their brilliant eyes following her everywhere she went. All of them had wires attached to their heads. All of them were no more than a year old. And, if Jennifer's plan succeeded, all of them would be free by this time tomorrow.

She leaned over the cot of the eldest baby, a little girl with a thick head of hair. "I'm not standing by while you get treated like guinea pigs," Jennifer whispered, fiercely. "Not anymore."

Jennifer had lied to Ted. She wasn't on his side. She would never be on his side again.

ROZ MACLAREN

Chapter One

It's funny how the most important moments in your life don't seem important at the time.

They should come with an announcement, or, better yet, a warning label. CAUTION: TREAT THIS MOMENT WISELY. FAILURE TO DO SO COULD RESULT IN SERIOUS INJURY. OR DEATH.

That's what should have happened when January Hill walked into my classroom. I should have at least gotten a heads-up that my life was about to change forever.

But, as is always the way, I had no reason to suspect anything out of the ordinary was happening, other than that a really pretty girl had walked into the room and was standing in front of us all, looking as if she would rather be anywhere else but here.

Even Earwig Carson sat up to look at her, and he's been going out with Karen Miles for the last two years. As soon as I saw Earwig looking at the new girl, I dropped my gaze. You didn't want to get on Earwig's wrong side. Rumor had it a kid had to change schools because Earwig didn't like his haircut. If you've never met Earwig, you'd probably think that was just a rumor. If you *have* met Earwig, you'd have no doubts that it was the truth. Anyway, you don't have to pay too much attention to Earwig. He's not the real villain of this story — he just thinks he is.

And I'm not the protagonist either. She is.

I risked another peek at her as she stood there. You know how they say some people walk into a room and light it up? That's exactly what she was doing. And not because she had a sunny personality or was all smiles or anything like that. She just *glowed*. I could almost feel an electrical charge in the air around her, like the faint crackle before a thunderstorm.

She was smaller than most girls in our year. Petite, I guess you'd say. You might even call her skinny. She wore a beret and all her hair must have been swept up under it because not even a strand of it was visible.

Ms. Mackenzie introduced her. "Everybody, I'd like you to meet January Hill. She'll be starting today."

January said nothing. She cast her eyes around the room like she was the gold champion of the Olympic staring contest. I was certain that girl could stare down a cobra.

Ms. Mackenzie was doing some staring of her own. "January, we don't allow hats in class. You've been told. Please take it off."

January seemed remarkably unfazed. She clearly didn't realize how ferocious Ms. Mackenzie could be. "It's for medical reasons. I get terrible head colds unless I wear a hat."

I smirked down at my desk. Yeah, right. I didn't consider myself to be the world's best judge of character, but even I knew January was lying. She probably wanted to keep the hat as some kind of fashion statement.

Ms. Mackenzie sighed, like it was an argument they'd had before. "Yes, and if you bring me a note from your doctor saying this, I'll allow a hat."

January's eyes narrowed. "I've literally just moved here. How do you expect me to bring a note?"

With exaggerated patience, Ms. Mackenzie said: "January. Here, students do not talk back to their teachers. They do exactly as they are told when they are told. And I am telling you. Remove. Your. Hat."

Things got dramatic fast. January's eyes seemed to be on fire as she glared at Ms. Mackenzie. "So, you're telling me I have to get a head cold because you won't accept that I don't even have a doctor yet, let alone a note from them?"

Ms. Mackenzie's eyes narrowed. "Remove your hat or remove yourself from my class."

"Oh." January smiled. "You didn't tell me I had a choice."

It was all over before most of us even processed it. January glided past us all, past the rows of gaping mouths and wide eyes, past the door, and made for the window. She flung it open and jumped out. We remained staring at the open window for several minutes and probably would still be staring at it if Ms. Mackenzie hadn't snapped: "Everyone, attention!" and tried her best to regain some authority.

"That girl is going to be trouble," my best friend, Sam, whispered to me.

I just smiled. I thought January was going to be fun.

****

January didn't come back to school the next day. I wasn't surprised. I wondered if she knew she'd set the whole school abuzz. Rumors were flying about her, about the black beret perched on her head, about the way she hadn't given a damn. Some said she was completely bald, some said she had a secret tattoo she didn't want the teachers seeing. Some said she was a grown-up who had escaped from prison and disguised herself as a schoolgirl. Even back then, I knew they were all wrong.

It was the weekend before I saw her again. She was wearing a top hat this time. Who wears a top hat in the middle of the supermarket? January Hill, apparently. A top hat, paired with a leather playsuit and knee-high boots. She was looking fiercely at the cat food, as if she wanted to set fire to it all.

My hands were sweating as I stuffed them in my

jeans pockets and tried to act casual. "Hey, January."

She turned and I got the force of her gaze directed at me. Let's just say I would hate to upset January. She had quite a glare going on. It softened slightly when she saw me. "Oh. Hi."

I realized she probably had no idea who I was. I decided to remind her. "You're in my class. Or, you were, before you jumped out the window."

Her cheeks reddened. "You know, that's the shortest I've ever lasted at school. Usually I get through the morning at least."

"Cute hat." I nodded in the direction of her looming top hat. "I liked the beret better though."

January shrugged, as if she really didn't care what my views on her headwear might be. "And you are?"

"Leon. Leon Marsh."

She swiped up a tin of cat food, nodded sharply at me, and began to walk away.

Think of something to say! I urged myself. *Don't just let her go.*

"So, um, you have a cat?" I asked her retreating back.

She turned and rolled her eyes. "No, this is for my supper. Yeah, I have a cat."

"What's she called?" I hurried to catch up with her.

"He. Clyde."

"Me and my friends hang out on the weekends. You could join us if you wanted." Did that sound casual enough? Probably not.

Casual or not, January wasn't interested. "Thanks, Marsh, but there's not a lot of point. I don't stick around many places long enough to make friends."

At that moment, a woman turned down the aisle, pushing a shopping cart. She smiled at January. "Making friends, dear?"

"No." January dumped the cat food in the trolley. "Later, Marsh."

The woman turned to me, pushing fair hair out of her eyes. "Hi. I'm Jess Hill, January's mom. Are you in January's class?"

I nodded. "Yeah, that's right. Leon Marsh."

Unlike January, her mom seemed to want to talk to me. "Is January settling in at school?"

I glanced at January, wondering if I should tell Mrs. Hill that January hadn't been at school long enough to learn my name, let alone settle in. January was looking at the floor, kicking at one of the tiles with her foot. She raised her eyes to mine. There was a challenge in them. *Well? Are you going to tell on me?*

"She's doing great," I lied. "She's really popular, everyone likes her…"

"Don't overdo it, Marsh," January advised. I thought I saw a flicker of gratitude in her eyes. And was that the ghost of a smile?

Jess smiled approvingly at her daughter and then turned back to me. "That's great to hear. Why don't you come over tonight? We're having a pizza night. January hasn't had anyone over since we moved here, and it would be nice for her to make some friends."

January's eyes were fixed on her mother. "Is that really a good idea?" she demanded.

Jess shot January a glance that I didn't quite understand. "It'll be fine, honey."

January scowled. "Well, Leon can't come tonight. He's busy doing homework. Aren't you?" She shot me a loaded glance, clearing wanting me to agree with her.

"Nope, done it all." I ignored January's glare and smiled instead at her mother. "Thanks, I'd love to."

And that is how I ended up at January Hill's house

at 5:40 PM on a Saturday night, wearing my best jeans, a ton of aftershave, and what I hoped was an engaging smile. (January later informed me I looked like I'd swallowed a hairball.)

January let me in and led me through to the kitchen. The smell of slightly burnt pizza met my nostrils. A black cat sashayed towards me, weaving through my legs. I bent to stroke it. "Hey, Clyde." I glanced at January to see if she was impressed I'd remembered her cat's name and got a quirk of an eyebrow in return. Boy, was this girl hard to read.

I was worried dinner would be awkward, with Jess asking me questions about what I wanted to be when I grew up, the way grown-ups do when they can't think of anything to say to a teenager, but it was actually okay. We all sat on the sofa, eating pizza off our knees. In the end, it was me asking Jess questions. "So, what do you do, Mrs. Hill?"

Jess hesitated. "I haven't got a job yet. I'll probably look for something in hospitality."

"Mom used to be a scientist," January said, proudly.

"Really? That's cool. Whereabouts?"

Jess shot January a loaded glance. "Oh, you don't want to talk about boring stuff like my work. Why don't we see what's on TV? What do you like to watch?" She didn't wait for me to answer, flicking through channels and settling on some game show. The canned laughter and the overly loud presenter drowned out further conversation.

After the pizza, we went up to January's bedroom. There was no way on earth my parents would have let me take a girl up to *my* bedroom. Not without listening outside the door. But Jess didn't seem to mind and she certainly wasn't hanging around at the keyhole. We left her in the living room, pouring herself another glass of wine.

"We're not friends," January snapped as soon as we were alone. "I told you, I don't want friends."

I shrugged. It wasn't what I wanted to hear, but at least it was honest. "What's wrong with having friends?"

"I told you. I move around too often to bother making friends. And you can make all the promises in the world and say you'll stay in touch, but you never do, and then one day, when I do come back, I'll find you've made friends with a girl called Kristen, and you're taking her to the Christmas party you said you'd take me to and then…" She tailed off. "Forget it."

"That was alarmingly specific." I stepped in front of her. "Listen, I'm not making any promises. I don't know anything about you. I might not want to keep in touch with you. But I don't know anyone called Kristen and I absolutely hate Christmas parties. So, on that basis, do you want to give being friends a shot?"

"If I have to." She sank down on the bed. "If I really have to."

I smiled. "Good enough."

Her room wasn't like I'd pictured. There were no posters of the boybands Karen Miles and her cronies worshipped.

Even though January hadn't been here long, the walls were filled with sketches. Pictures of January, her hair glowing red, orange, blue, green, different in every picture. Sketches of people I didn't know, places I'd never seen.

"You draw, then?" I asked.

"Yeah. A bit." January picked at the skin around her nails, eyes glued to the floor.

"You're good."

"Thanks." This was the first time she'd got close

to a smile. I liked it.

"So how come you're not wearing a hat in any of these pictures?" I peered at her self-portraits, at the way her hair looked almost like a living thing.

January's voice was unexpectedly bitter. "I hate hats."

I frowned. "How come you wouldn't take it off that day in class then?"

She glared at me. "If we're going to be friends, you'd better get one thing inside your head. Don't ask me any questions."

Waves of frustration and anger barreled through me. I'd tried really hard to be nice to this girl. But she clearly didn't want anything to do with me, and maybe it was time I respected her wishes. "Forget it." I stood up. "That's not friendship on any level and if that's how you're going to be, then maybe it's just as well you move around so much because you certainly aren't going to fit in here."

"Yeah, maybe it is!" January yelled back. "And maybe you should get out my room and go back where you came from!"

"Don't worry, I'm going!" *Not* my best comeback, as parting shots go, but the best I could do at that moment. I was too annoyed to think of something more cutting.

I took the stairs two at a time and slammed the door behind me. I made up my mind I would never speak to January Hill again.

Chapter Two

A single hair can hold up to 100 grams in weight. An entire head of hair could hold the equivalent of two elephants.

Here's the thing about me. I like facts. The more obscure, the better. I've never lost a single game of Trivial Pursuit. To the point that when I tried to play it with my friends, they groaned and refused. I couldn't help it—I liked knowing stuff. (Looking back, it probably wasn't surprising I've never had a girlfriend.)

My mom couldn't understand me. She never said as much—at least, not to me—but she looked at me like I was strange subspecies. I think, in her mind, all boys were obsessed with girls, football, and cars. I couldn't stand football. I liked cars about as much as the next boy. And girls … well, they were just *there* really. We had one girl in our gang, but the rest were too cool to bother with us. I had the usual posters of film stars up on my wall, but that was mainly an act of defiance because my dad had long ago told me I couldn't have posters. Apparently the pins marked the wall. The day after he left, I bought a box of push-pins and punctured my bedroom walls all over. After all, why not? I felt like he had punctured me all over.

Sam, Ginger, James, and I spent our Sundays fishing, or trying to. I don't think we ever caught anything more exciting than old boots. I didn't care. I didn't really like the idea of killing fish, but I didn't want to say so in front of the guys.

"I am so ready for summer vacation," sighed Ginger. Meet Ginger Monroe. Sixteen, small, scientific, geeky, with long red hair. "Just one more week of school and then freedom…" She wiggled her toes in the water.

"Stop scaring the fish off, Ginger," growled

James. The rebel in our group. Leather jacket, even in the height of summer. Enough hair gel to keep a barber's shop supplied for months. Pierced ear and even a tattoo, though God knows how he convinced any tattoo artist he was old enough to get one.

And then me and Sam. Best friends since we were toddlers, so our moms told us. Met at nursery and bonded over finger painting and a shared love of orange juice. I couldn't remember a time when Sam hadn't been in my life. Sam, with his floppy brown hair and his failed attempt to grow a beard ("There's stubble there, Leon, I swear it." "Yeah, in your dreams, Sammy.") and his uncanny ability to always know if something was wrong with me. If I was even slightly off, Sam would never let it drop until I told him what was wrong.

And he knew that day something was wrong. Because, no matter how much I lied to myself, I really did want to be friends with January Hill. Maybe more than friends, if I was being really, truly honest. Nobody quite like her had ever come to our town. Nobody had ever rocked up with crazy hats and defiant eyes, nobody had ever climbed out a window and walked away from a teacher, nobody had ever *not cared* the way she did.

"I'm going home," I said. "I'm sick of not catching any fish."

They looked at me like I'd said I was going to the moon. "But we never catch any fish. It's like the summer tradition."

"Yeah, well, maybe I'm bored of it."

"Wait for me." Sam was beside me. "I'll walk with you."

I did a mental countdown. I got to ten before he asked me what was wrong, just exactly as I knew he would.

"I was at January Hill's last night," I said. "She's

a nasty piece of work."

Sam burst out laughing. "Oh, wow, you *like* her, don't you?"

"'Course not." I didn't know why I was wasting my time trying to deny it. People like Sam can't be lied to. They always know.

"Yeah you do. You should ask her out sometime."

I snorted. Like January would ever want to do that. "Never going to happen. I told you, she's nasty."

"Speak of the devil…" Sam pointed into the distance.

January. Wearing a beanie perched on her head and one of those tops that you tie in the middle. I was right, she was skinny. Stomach so flat you could probably have laid her down and played pool on her. Denim shorts with a ragged edge that looked like she'd just decided one day she wanted shorts and cut her jeans to shreds. She hadn't seen us. Her attention was fixed on someone else. Instinctively, we turned to follow her gaze.

"Crap, it's Earwig!" hissed Sam.

Meet Gary "Earwig" Carson. Seventeen years old, taller than most of his teachers. The kind of guy who could get sent out of Hell for bad behavior. If you were in trouble with Earwig, your best bet was leaving the country, growing a beard, and changing your name. And, even then, he'd probably still find you.

"Let's hide, he might not spot us." Sam dragged me behind a tree before I had a chance to think.

Earwig was walking in the other direction. January was still a good distance away as she walked towards him. And, also walking towards Earwig but far closer to him was a kid of about ten years old, a bag of something in his hand.

"That kid's in for it," groaned Sam. "That's Billy Jones' brother, isn't it? Little Tommy?"

"Think so."

Earwig was looming over Tommy. "What's that you've got there?"

"Um … candy?"

"I can see that, you idiot. What kind?"

"Chocolate," murmured Tommy indistinctly through a mouthful of candy.

Earwig smiled. It wasn't a pleasant sight. "My favorite."

"They're mine," Tommy said, as if he was trying to convince himself more than Earwig.

Earwig snatched them out of Tommy's hand and held them in the air. "And now they're mine."

"Hey!" All eyes turned towards her. She was a flash of lightning. She was a tornado. She was a meteor. She was heading straight for Earwig. "Give that boy back his candy, you monster."

"Or what?" spat Earwig. "What's a pipsqueak like you going to do about it?"

"We have to help her!" I hissed at Sam.

"What? No! Then we'll all be in trouble with Earwig and then we'll have to leave the country and then…" I clamped my hand over Sam's mouth to silence his garbled babbling.

Actually, January didn't seem in need of any help. She was glaring at Earwig and he was glaring at her. And she definitely wasn't backing down.

Earwig took a step closer to January. "You're new in town. So I'll be generous. I'll give you the chance to walk away and we can forget all this ever happened."

"Yes," mumbled Sam beside me, my hand still clamped over his mouth. "Walk away, walk away!"

January wasn't walking away. "I'm not afraid of you and I'm not going anywhere."

Earwig's eyebrows shot up. Probably in surprise. I

couldn't honestly remember anyone ever telling Earwig they weren't afraid of him. His own parents treated him with a healthy caution. The teachers were definitely afraid of him. He'd had a growth spurt last year and stood about six feet tall. Add to that all the hours he spent in the gym, pumping iron, and the guy had developed enough strength to crush the likes of me and Sam like bugs. And January ... well, she was even smaller than us.

"Turn and go," ordered Earwig. "Or I'll show you just how scary I can be." He loomed above January, snarling down at her. His fists were clenched and for one, terrible moment, I thought he was going to hit her.

January just smiled, like she had everything under control. "Unfortunately for you, I don't scare easily."

And this is the part in the story where you're going to have to pay attention. You're going to have to trust me. Because I could tell this story a thousand times and nobody would believe me. I wouldn't have believed it myself if I hadn't seen it.

January pulled off her beanie and masses of brilliant red hair tumbled down. I'd never seen hair quite so long, extending past her waist. But it was the color that was so mesmerizing. Is there such a shade as electric red? I know there's electric blue. And electric is the only word I can think of to describe her hair. Dazzling. Almost glowing. Almost alive.

And then a tendril of that brilliant red hair reached up for the bag of candy, snatched it out Earwig's grasp, and put it back in Tommy's hand.

It was all over in the blink of an eye. And Sam and I did a lot of blinking, because surely ... surely our eyes were deceiving us. January Hill did not just hand the chocolates back to Tommy with her hair. Did she?

"Scram!" she said, sharply, to Tommy—and he ran, little legs flying.

Earwig was staring at her. "How the hell did you do that?"

"Do what? Take candy from a wimp like you and give them back to their rightful owner? It wasn't particularly hard." January turned to go.

For a split second, I had a flicker of hope. Hope that she might just have got away with it. That Earwig might have been so taken by surprise, he would let her go.

But he shot out a muscular arm and grabbed her wrist, pulling her backwards and bending it at an impossible angle.

"Get off me, creepo," she snapped.

Earwig laughed in her face. "Not until you tell me how you did that trick."

Was it my imagination or was her hair changing color? Still predominantly red, but with a steady hint of orange creeping through it?

"Let go of me," she snapped. "I'm warning you."

"Hey, Earwig!" I jumped up. "Get the hell away from her! Leave her alone."

Behind me, Sam muttered, "Leon, you idiot!"

"Oh, great, it's the January Fan Club." Earwig rolled his eyes, but didn't release his grip on her.

I have no idea what my plan was, just so you know. Did I hope that running up to Earwig would terrorize him so badly he let January go? The guy was at least a foot taller than me and a whole year older. He was only in my class because he'd been held back. There was no way I'd be able to intimidate someone like him. I realized that when I got up to him and he was standing there, towering over both of us and laughing. I could see saliva stringing between his teeth as he opened his mouth. It looked like he was gearing up to eat us, like some monster in a children's picture book.

"Oh, for goodness' sake." January tossed her hair like she was bored of the situation. Her hair snaked up Earwig's arm, curling and curving like a vine around a tree. I watched, hypnotized, as it reached his shoulder, then around his neck.

"Get it off me, get it off me!" He flapped at it with his free hand. "Get it the hell off me, you evil witch!"

"Let me go then." A smile flickered on January's lips.

Earwig remembered who he was. Earwig Carson did not let people go. Ever. He tightened his grip on January's wrist.

"Your funeral." She smiled at him, and I could see the twists of her hair tighten around his throat.

Earwig clawed at her hair with both his hands, turning a highly unattractive shade of purple. "You're choking me, you're choking me," he croaked.

January's hair tightened one last time and then released. Earwig dropped to his knees, coughing. He was struggling to his feet when a wall of scarlet hair hit him hard in the face. Picture a tidal wave. Picture a bulldozer. You're close to imagining the force that hit Earwig. He was knocked onto his back and January stamped her foot on his chest, pinning him down.

"Scram," ordered January. "And remember this moment when you pick on little kids."

Earwig scrammed. I had never seen Earwig scram before, so I savored the moment. My savoring took place mostly open-mouthed.

Sam crept out from behind the tree. "Did he just...?"

"Yep."

"And did she...?"

We both turned to stare at January. She rolled her eyes. "Right, well, obviously you weren't meant to see that. Why were you two stalkers hiding behind a tree in the first place?"

"Earwig avoidance tactics," I said.

"You guys are scared of that punk?" January's voice rose in surprise, as if Earwig was no more than a minor irritation and she was shocked that anyone would be in fear of him.

"Hello!" Sam waved frantically in her face. "We don't all have magic hair! Earwig once used a football net to tie me up and locked me in a cupboard at school for, like, three days." (It was actually two hours, but I didn't think Sam would appreciate me correcting him.) "Wish I had magic hair."

"Shh! Will you keep it down!" January gathered her hair up and slammed her beanie back on top, glancing over her shoulder nervously. "If you two ever tell anyone what you saw, I will creep into your bedrooms and strangle you in your sleep."

"We won't tell," I said.

Sam nodded. "Yeah, obviously. We can keep a secret."

January smiled, almost sadly. "The good thing about this secret is no one would believe you anyway."

Chapter Three

Your heart beats around 100,000 times a day.

Unless you're with January Hill, in which case, it's double that figure.

Especially if you've just witnessed her choke someone with her own hair.

Considering the situation, I'd say an increased heartbeat was a very normal reaction to have and nothing whatsoever to do with the fact that I may or may not have had a crush on her.

James and Ginger came sprinting up. "We saw Earwig running off like he'd seen a ghost! What happened?"

Sam pointed at January. "She happened. She has magic hair."

January folded her arms. "Oh great, now everyone knows."

Ginger's nose wrinkled in confusion. "Magic hair?" she echoed, at the same time as James spluttered "Magic hair? Yeah right."

"It's true," I said.

"How … how did you get like that?" Sam was stuttering, still looking at January. He does that when he's nervous or excited. In this case, he was probably both.

January sighed. "I don't know. It's been like this as long as I can remember."

Sam's eyes were so wide, I thought they were going to pop out of his head. "Is it just the hair on your head that's magic or … other body hair too?"

"Sam, don't be gross," I snapped.

"What?" he blinked at me. "I'm just asking what you're thinking."

"I can assure you, that is *not* what I was thinking!" I protested. (Although *now* it was definitely what I was thinking.)

"Can we just drop it please?" January asked. "I really don't want to talk about my hair. I shouldn't have done that with Earwig. Probably means we're going to have to move again." She kicked at the ground with the toe of her trainer. "I was kind of liking it here. Even though it's boring and all." She flashed me a glance. "No offence."

None taken. If you've got magic hair, then I imagine most normal stuff seems boring.

"So, is that why you keep moving? In case people find out about your hair?" I asked. It was starting to make sense. Her total reluctance to get attached to people. The way she hadn't given a damn about making a good impression at school.

January straightened her hat. "Yeah. I don't usually lose my temper like that, but that kid Earwig is a pain. How do you guys put up with him?"

"Stay the heck out his way," Ginger said. "He supposedly almost drowned a kid in the showers one day at school, just because he said the kid looked at him for too long."

"Sounds a charmer."

Sam nodded wildly. "Seriously, you don't make an enemy out of Earwig. Not if you want to stay alive."

"Sam, relax," I said. "She practically killed him. I don't think he'll be giving her any trouble."

"Will he tell anyone, do you think?" January was chewing her lip.

"What, that he was beaten by a girl?" I laughed. "Earwig would rather die than have anyone know what happened today. Don't worry, he'll keep his trap shut."

January visibly relaxed. "Look, I'm sorry I was so horrible to you before," she said to me.

My heart was doing this annoying slamming

against my chest. *Get it together, Leon. Just because the girl you like is finally talking to you like you're a human being and not something nasty she wants to scrape off the bottom of her shoes, you don't have to go all to pieces.* "It's fine. Listen, how about you hang out with us? You can be part of our gang. Me and Sam and Ginger and James."

James' eyes were practically burning a hole in my face. "Leon, can I have a word?" He pulled me to one side. "We only have one girl in the gang, and we don't invite anyone to join without running it past everyone first!"

"This is a special occasion!" I hissed.

"Why? Because you *like* her?" asked Sam.

"Shut up!" I clamped my hand over his mouth for the second time that day, glancing over my shoulder to make sure January hadn't heard. My cheeks burned. I wanted her in our gang desperately. I wanted any reason to be near her. *Think, Leon, you've gotta find some way to persuade the guys.* And then it hit me. "This girl is our ticket to freedom." I folded my arms, letting my words sink in. "Think about it. She's already terrified Earwig. So if he sees us with her, he'll leave us alone. And you know what that means?"

Sam's brow furrowed. "Not really…"

"It means, idiot, we rule the school."

"Oh wow!" He pushed his glasses up his nose. "I suppose we do! Take Earwig out and there's a vacancy at the top of the food chain."

"At the very least, we get a scare-free summer." I ran a hand through my hair, trying to look casual, and not like I'd just thought all that up on the spot.

James looked at me, musingly. With a shrug, he said, "All right, deal. She can join."

We turned back to look at January and found her

standing directly behind us.

"Jeez, don't creep up on people like that!" Sam exclaimed.

And then we stared. We stared like our eyes were going to fall out our heads. Her incredible hair had been red when last looked. Now, it was an explosion of pink waves, tumbling down her shoulders.

"I'm not going mad, am I?" Ginger checked. "It was red a minute ago, wasn't it?"

"It changes color," January muttered.

"That is so damn cool!" Sam gawped. Literal gawpage. No other way to describe it.

"Can you control it?" I asked. "The color thing."

January shook her head. "It'll change depending on what mood I'm in."

"So red earlier because you were angry?" I guessed. "And then it turned orange when you argued with Earwig."

January nodded. "It goes orange when I'm scared. And, in spite of what I said to him, that dude was a bit scary."

"And what does pink mean?" demanded Ginger.

"It means I'm embarrassed, okay?" snapped January. "Do you want a printout of all the colors my hair goes when my mood swings? Maybe I'll do you all some leaflets so you can read them instead of staring at me!"

I touched her arm. "Hey." When she looked at me, I said, "We're your friends."

She bit her lip so hard I thought it would start bleeding. "I've never had friends before," she muttered.

"I'm honestly not surprised," James said.

January lifted her head to stare at him. My palms started to sweat. Would she choke him? Do that hair slap thing?

A sound came out of January that I had never

heard before. It started low, like a cat's growl, and then got louder. It took me a few seconds to realize she was laughing. And her hair was now blue. Whatever that meant.

The tension melted away. January was one of us.

Everyone was suddenly talking all at once. Ginger cornered January and was asking her if her hair had a mind of its own or if she controlled it. Sam and James were arguing about their plans for summer vacation.

Me? Well, I guess that's the other thing you'll have to learn about me. If January's superpower is magic hair, then I think mine is invisibility. Because, sometimes, I swear people don't see me even when I'm right in front of them.

This isn't going to be some pity party story, so don't worry. Like I said, I've got a best friend and two other good friends. I'm luckier than the kids who don't have any friends and who get picked on all the time. If I disappeared it would take everyone at least a week before they realized. Even Sam.

Then January lifted her head and turned. Her eyes searched until they found mine. And I felt something jump inside my chest.

Maybe, just maybe, January would be the one to see me. Invisible or not.

ROZ MACLAREN

Chapter Four

It is physically impossible for pigs to look up at the sky.

This has always made me sad. The kind of ache you get inside, that you can't explain. The kind that physically hurts. Like when it rains all summer vacation and you can't go out and hang with your friends and you just stand at the window watching raindrops wriggle down the glass. That kind of melancholy mixed with yearning.

I was ten when I read that about pigs. I actually started crying. (Yeah, I know. I was a baby.) I just thought of how it would feel to be a pig and never see a blue sky. Never know what that yellow thing is that shines down on me. Never see the stars or the moon or a plane or even birds.

I feel like that pig, sometimes. Like there's a whole world of activity going on right over my head, but I'm out of it. I can't even look at it, let alone join in.

I used to be able to look up at the sky. My dad bought me a telescope when I was ten. Not one of those tiny little brass ones you see in antique shops. A massive one that needed a tripod to hold it up. One that showed every crater on the moon.

We put it in the attic under the skylight. Whenever I couldn't sleep, I'd go up there and look for hours at the sparkling stars in the ink-black sky. My dad tried to teach me the names of all the stars and constellations, but I can only remember Orion now. And that's only because, when I was little, I misheard my dad and thought it was called "Leon." Yep, you guessed it—I was dumb enough to think they'd named a constellation after me. I was heartbroken when I found out I'd got it wrong. Don't laugh—I was only eight.

It used to be so easy to talk to him when we were sitting there, in the dark. I could tell him about scary dreams I'd had, about the girl I liked in school, about how I was worried I'd fail math. We'd had so many conversations thanks to that telescope.

He took it with him when he left. His new kid probably looks through it now.

I've never looked through a telescope since.

Sorry. I said it wasn't going to be a pity party story, and that's how it's turning out.

I'd stick around for the rest though, if I were you. This is where it gets exciting.

**** .

We should have known Earwig would tell Karen. He tells Karen everything.

It was the last day of school. January didn't bother to turn up. "It's hardly worth it, is it?" she had smiled, when I brought it up. "I might come back if we're still here when it starts again."

But she was there to meet us on our last day. Standing there, wearing a ragged-edged skirt with red and black stripy tights. She wore a corset, black lace gloves, and a trilby hat. I thought she looked incredibly otherworldly, like she'd stepped off the pages of a storybook.

"Freak!" someone called.

She just smiled. Her eyes were locked on mine. "Welcome to freedom."

"Thanks." I nodded at her skirt. "Nice outfit."

"Yeah, nice outfit for freaks." Karen Miles was behind me, accompanied by her lapdog, Brooke.

Karen Miles. The kind of face you'd expect to see on the pages of a glossy magazine, but with all the charisma and intelligence of an adder. Never seen without

Brooke Cox, a vapid and unimaginative follower. If they lived in medieval times, Brooke would be Karen's handmaiden, the one who does the dirty work while Karen shines. I wished they did live in medieval times. Any time other than my time would have been perfect.

"Get lost, Karen," I snapped. "I'm talking to my friend."

"Your 'friend' has bizarre taste in fashion." Karen used air quotes when she said "fashion." "Honestly, where did you get your outfit from? A dumpster?"

January ignored her, looping her arm through mine. "Good day at school?"

"Same old." We walked away, Karen and Brooke trailing after us. I groaned internally. I really didn't want this, not today. "Look, can you two just go and take a long walk off a short pier?" I snapped. "Leave us alone."

"Girls like her aren't welcome here." Karen stabbed a finger in January's direction. "She's some kind of witch. Do you know what they used to do to witches in the old days?" She stood right in front of January. "They burned them."

"Is that supposed to frighten me?" January raised her eyebrows.

"My boyfriend told me all about you." Karen refused to back down. "Personally, I think they should take you away and lock you up."

I choked back a laugh. "Seriously, Karen, get lost."

Karen looked at me. "Do you know what she did to Earwig? She terrorized him!"

"Good," I found myself saying. "Makes a change from Earwig doing the terrorizing. Run along, now, Karen."

"Not until she apologizes." Karen stabbed a finger in January's direction, her bangles jangling.

"I don't know what you're talking about," January said. "Let's go, Leon."

Karen caught hold of January's wrists. "I'm warning you, January."

"I'm so scared," she mocked.

Brooke laughed. "You should be."

I don't think any of us saw it coming. There was a flash of silver as Karen's bangles caught the light and then crack! Her palm made contact with January's cheek. January just stood there blinking at her for a second. Her cheek was turning scarlet.

"Right, that's enough, Karen!" I started pulling her arm, trying to drag her away. I wasn't quick enough.

January's Trilby was on the ground and her hair was winding its way along Karen's wrists, forcing her arms above her head. January's face was inches from Karen's as she hissed: "Leave me the hell alone."

In one powerful movement, January's wave of bright red hair had pushed Karen to the ground.

Karen was laughing. "Congratulations, January. You just made the biggest mistake of your life." She marched off, her sidekick in tow.

January replaced her hat. "I need to stop doing that," she muttered.

"Why? It's seriously cool." Did I sound too eager? Did I sound like I was crushing on her? Oh, probably.

She shot me a look. "You know why."

I tried to reassure her. "Don't worry, they've got the whole summer to forget about what happened. It's just 'cause you hurt Earwig's pride. Come on. The others will be waiting for us."

You know in books where people have a feeling of premonition? Or something happens to them and they realize, without knowing why, that this was an Important

Moment? Yeah, I didn't have that. Because if I was subject to premonitions, I'd have had some indication that this was the moment that was going to change everything. Or maybe I'd have seen what Brooke Cox was doing behind us. I would have turned around and maybe football tackled her to the ground and snatched her phone out of her hands and that would have solved everything. I would have deleted the video she'd just recorded and January would have looked at me like I was a hero and everything that happened afterwards would have gone differently.

But me being me, I didn't do any of those things. And I just walked along the road with January, oblivious to the danger we were now in.

ROZ MACLAREN

Chapter Five

The average person spends almost ten hours online—spending more time on the Internet than they do sleeping.
Especially so if you lived in our town, where the Internet speed could be measured in single figures.

Every now and then, I went on my dad's socials. Just to see how he was. What he was doing. Because he certainly wasn't going to tell me himself.

The last time he emailed me was three years ago. And that was to wish me a happy birthday. Five days late.

I sometimes wondered where the line between being in someone's life and being completely forgotten starts and ends. How can you be so close to someone one minute and then never hear from them the next? Was I really that easy to forget?

Must have been. His picture-perfect, camera-ready life showed him with his new wife, Suzanne, and her daughter, Meredith. And the new baby, Cleo. I hated the way my dad looked so comfortable with his new family. His hand casually resting on Meredith's shoulders, while he held the baby in his other arm and smiled at his wife. You'd look at them and say that was what happiness looked like. Three toothy smiles and one sleeping baby. That was the perfect family right there.

And I wasn't in it.

He left us when I was twelve. Moved out, took everything with him. I remember walking into the bedroom the day after. It was like someone had decorated half the room and forgotten about the other half. My mom's bedside table was filled with her usual junk, books, clock, tablet, glass of water. Dad's side was bare. Something about seeing the room that way made my skin crawl. Like it was some kind of modern art installation, titled The Divorce. Except, it was real and it was in my house and I couldn't get away from all the bare spaces my father had left behind. I didn't go back in their bedroom for a while.

I sometimes wondered why, when he wiped the entire room clean, when he took everything he owned and quite a few things he didn't, did he not take me?

****

January's cat lay on her pillow, every so often rumbling out a creaky purr. January was sketching him, her pencil effortlessly skimming over the page. I liked to watch her when she was concentrating. I liked to see her mind working, the way she was lost to the real world and entirely focused on what she was drawing. I wasn't sure she even remembered I was in the room. It made me feel both invisible and also part of something bigger, like I got to see a side of January nobody else did. Her long hair hung down over her shoulders in soft shades of blue and the tip of her tongue protruded between her lips as she concentrated.

"Can I see?" I asked when she had finished.

She hesitated and then chucked me her sketchbook. "There's a lot of trash in there."

I started at the beginning, flicking through pages of scenery I didn't recognize from places I had never been. For the first time, I realized just how often January had moved. Halfway through the book was the drawing of a man I didn't know. Surely he was far too old for January to have a crush on him? I stared at him, trying to work out if he was some kind of celebrity she'd just decided to draw. Maybe he was her grandad? He certainly looked like somebody's uncle. He had wisps of grey hair and wobbly jowls disappearing straight into his neck. A spider's web pattern of wrinkles collected around his eyes. January had captured him so well, it looked like he was staring right at me. The cold look in his dark eyes made my skin crawl.

"Who's this?" I asked, holding the sketchpad up.

January sighed. She was silent for so long, I thought she wasn't going to answer me. Then she crossed to her desk and pulled out a photograph of the man. "I found this in Mom's papers," she muttered. "I think … I think he might be my dad." She sat down beside me on the bed, the warmth of her body radiating towards me. "Jess isn't my birth mom," she confessed.

My eyebrows rose in surprise. I had vaguely wondered why there was no real resemblance between January and Jess. "Wow."

"She never told me anything about my birth parents," January continued. "I'm not sure if she even knows who they are. But when I found this photo, I thought maybe that guy was my dad. I sort of borrowed it and Mom never seemed to miss it so I just kept it. I've no idea if I'm his daughter or not but it … I don't know. It makes me feel better to think that maybe I am."

I nodded, pretending I understood. I *wanted* to understand. But then January didn't seem to understand the glaringly obvious: that dads who abandon you are far more trouble than they're worth and you're better off without them. Or maybe that was just true of my dad. Sorry, there I go, making it all about me again. But maybe some of it *is* about me. Because, when I flipped through to the end of the sketchbook, I saw myself.

I was walking down the road, hands in my pockets. Dust rose in swirling clouds on either side of me. I was looking at the ground, but I was smiling. One of my hands was in my hair, smoothing it down. I have mud-brown hair but January had darkened it in the drawing, making it look like it was the color of shadows. Most of

January's drawings were in black and white, but, for some reason, she had chosen to capture me in color. My eyes were deep blue, the brightest thing about me, sparkling with something that looked a lot like happiness. January had portrayed me in a way I never knew anyone saw me. I looked cool. I looked like someone I'd want to be friends with.

I looked up at her. A faint blush was spreading across her nose and cheeks.

"You drew me?"

She shrugged. I expected a snarky reply but she just said, "That's how you look when you forget to be sad and you live in the moment."

"I'm not sad," I protested.

January raised an eyebrow. "Flip forward."

I flicked through the pages. I saw myself, staring back at myself. Eyes dark and moody. Face half in shadow. A half smile that somehow looked sadder than no smile. If that was really what I looked like, then no wonder January thought I was sad. But all I could think was *January Hill drew me. January Hill looked at me.* And not just looked at me but looked deep into my soul. I glanced up at her. She was still looking at me, her face so close I could feel the faint whisper of her breath on my cheek.

"That's how you look when you think no one else is watching, Leon," she said, softly.

"But you were."

A twist of a smile appeared on her lips. "I guess we're both used to going unseen."

"Do you ever want to find your birth parents?" I asked, tentatively. Even after a few weeks of hanging out, I still wasn't sure where I stood with January. Some questions made her flip out, some made her clam up, and I never knew what I was allowed to ask and what I wasn't.

January shrugged. "Maybe. I know this guy has something to do with my birth." She flicked back through the sketchbook and tapped her pencil on the old dude's face. "I tried asking Mom about it once but she got really upset and refused to talk about it. From the papers I sneaked a look at, I think she used to work with this guy when she was a scientist. But I don't know. I just know that every time I ask Mom about it, she cries. So I stopped asking."

ROZ MACLAREN

Chapter Six

You are more likely to die on your birthday than any other day.

The day my life exploded into a million little pieces certainly felt like any other day. It definitely wasn't my birthday. The only noteworthy thing about it was that it was recorded as our region's hottest day of the summer.

If I'd known what was going to happen, I'd have hugged my mother one last time. I'd have told her I was sorry I was such a pain after dad left. I'd have told her I knew really it wasn't her fault, that dad was the way he was because he chose to be. Then again, maybe I didn't know that at the time.

You could see the heat rising from the ground as the four us sat with our feet in the water. We weren't fishing that day—we were waiting for Ginger and January to come out of the corner shop before going to explore the woods.

The thing I remember most is the heat melting the tar in the road, leaking its licorice-like smell into my lungs.

"The girls are late," complained James.

"January's not that bad, is she?" I checked. "You both like her, yeah?"

"She's sort of cool," admitted Sam.

"Yeah, she's okay," agreed James, with a shrug of his shoulders.

"I wish she'd do more with her hair though," Sam said. "I mean, she's got frigging superpowers and she never uses them."

"They're not exactly superpowers," I chipped in.

Sam rolled his eyes. "Bro. She saw off Earwig

and Karen with just her hair! She's practically a superhero."

James smirked. "She's Leon's girlfriend, so don't get any ideas, Sam."

"She is *not* my girlfriend," I spluttered.

"Except in your dreams maybe." Sam jogged my arm.

"Get lost, Sam," I growled. He punched me playfully in the arm and I got him in a headlock.

"Guys…" Something in James' tone made me look up. Three men were walking down our street. That, in itself, was quite unusual. If there was an award for sleepy villages where nothing ever happens, ours would win every time. Even more unusual was the fact that I didn't recognize the men. I'd lived here all my life. I knew everyone, whether I wanted to or not, because that's just the way it was in a small town. And I had never seen these guys before in my life.

"Wow, who the hell are they?" I asked

"They're just men." Sam said, clearly anxious to get back to kicking my ass.

"Yeah, but look at them," James said.

There was nothing distinctive about them, and yet, at the same time, they stuck out. They were all three tall and burly, built like wrestlers. And all of them wore suits, in spite of the blazing sun.

"They're probably just on vacation," I shrugged, slyly punching Sam while he was distracted.

Ginger and January came out of the shops, both of them juggling ice cream cones. January had a sun hat and shades on, looking like a film star in her crop top and shorts. Ginger was starting to burn in the summer heat, her skin turning an angry red. Even so, she looked kinda cute (though not as cute as January and also I could never voice this thought as Ginger was James' girlfriend). The men also seemed to think she looked striking, as they turned to stare at her as she walked by. Her hair looked like liquid fire in the bright sunshine. One of them said something to the other and then they called to Ginger. "Hey, kid."

Ginger turned. "Um, yeah?"

"Could you give us directions to the main street?" Their accents told me they definitely weren't from around here.

January's eyes were hidden behind her sunglasses, but something about her body language made the hairs on the back of my neck stand up. She wasn't comfortable. She didn't trust these men. So neither did I. Before I really knew what I was doing, I'd pulled my feet out of the water, stuffed them in my shoes, and started to walk towards her.

"Um, this is the main street." Ginger was saying, as she gestured at the corner shop and the tiny street. She swept her long red hair out of her eyes. "There's not much else in this town."

"This is our map." One of the men got closer to Ginger and unfolded a map almost as big as a tablecloth. "And this is…"

At that moment, two things happened—in a split second. A van sped up towards the men. Its side door was slid open and the three men snatched Ginger up as if she weighed no more than a rag doll.

"Hey!" screamed January from the bottom of her lungs. "Let her go!" She ran at the men, but they shoved her away. The men bundled Ginger in the van, slamming the door shut behind them.

I was running now, running as fast as I could, but the van was already speeding off, leaving nothing but a cloud of dust. It was all over in the blink of an eye.

Ginger's ice cream lay in the road, already

melting into bittersweet trickles.

Chapter Seven

Sarcasm is said to boost creativity.

"What the actual hell just happened?" demanded Sam, like any of us had the answers.

We'd played games like this before, where one of us was kidnapped and the rest of us had to find them. In those games, we'd acted like heroes. We'd been brave, defiant in the face of danger. Fearless.

I guess I'd assumed that's how we would be if something like that happened in real life. But we weren't. None of us could move. We just stood there, burbling at each other.

James was the first to recover. "We need to get after them! They've kidnapped Ginger!"

"Yeah, James, we can all frigging see that," Sam snapped. "What do you suppose we do, run after them? They're in a van, by the way! And even if we catch them, do you want to just ask them to let Ginger go? Oh, yeah, they'd definitely listen to a bunch of teenage boys."

"And a girl with superpowers!" James reminded him. "We'll take my car and get after them."

In spite of our misgivings, we didn't have any better ideas. Reluctantly, we hurried to James' car.

****

On the outskirts of town, there was an abandoned mill. The owners of it once had a booming textile business, but, somewhere along the way, fell out over something and then disagreed over how they should use the mill. As a result, it had been left to go to rack and ruin long before we were born. We used to play in it before the owners got annoyed at having kids in their mill and boarded up the windows. Even so, when we were older and James somehow got hold of a crowbar, we'd gone in and he'd spraypainted things on the walls ("EARWIG IS

A [REDACTED]" and "GINGER AND JAMES 4EVA"). Eventually, the owners got even more annoyed and called our parents, who gave us all a stern talking-to and made us promise not to go in there again. We'd kept our promise. None of us had been there in years. In fact, I think most people had forgotten the mill ever existed. It was the perfect place for kidnappers to keep someone prisoner. And that's exactly where the kidnappers went. As James drove slowly after them (with Sam yelling at him not to get too close and me screaming that he was going to lose them if he didn't keep them in sight and James shouting at both of us to shut up and let him concentrate), their van pulled off the road and into the old mill's overgrown carpark. The road became a track, overgrown with thick weeds that slapped against the underneath of James' car. Trees formed a cavernous tunnel either side of the road, branches whipping the windscreen as the car crawled forwards.

Sam called the police. I think it was his first time ever dialing emergency services, because his voice went all high and squeaky and he wasn't making much sense. When he hung up, he said, "They said they'll be here as soon as they can."

"That could be ages." James looked at January. "Can you take them out?"

She looked blankly at him. "The men with guns! Can you take them out?"

"James, she's a girl, not a tank," I hissed.

"Maybe," January murmured. "I don't know. I'd need to get a closer look."

"Then let's go." James got out the car and strode over to the mill like he didn't care if the kidnappers saw him or not. We followed, reluctantly.

"This is madness," muttered Sam. "Why can't we just sit and wait for the police to get here?"

We all ignored him as we slipped to the back of the mill. James pointed above us to a boarded-up window and slowly we stood up and peered through the crack. It took a minute for our eyes to adjust to the darkness of the room—and we had to shuffle about to peer through the thick curtain of cobwebs on the other side.

Eventually, I could make out a chair with Ginger tied to it. Two of the men were leaning over her. One of them had a gun.

"Can you hear what they're saying?" demanded James. "Supergirl? Can you?"

"It's my hair that's magical, not my ears!" snapped January. "But I could hear more if you would shut the hell up!"

"We *all* need to shut up. What if they find us? And kill us?" quavered Sam.

It's always struck me as ironic. The very second the words were out Sam's mouth, a man rounded the corner. His gun was pointed straight at us.

"I thought I heard something back here," he said, smiling a toothless grin. His eyes met January's and he stared fixedly at her. A thin tendril of hair slipped out from under her hat. It was bright orange. "Show me your hair. And be quick about it, or I'll shoot your friends." Wordlessly, January pulled off her hat and let her hair tumble down. It was the color of tangerines and epic sunsets. It was the color of fear. The man's grin widened. "I knew it. *You're* the girl we want." He rapped hard on the boarded-up window. "That's the wrong kid."

"What?" yelled back one of the other men. A note of frustration crept into his voice. "What the hell do we do with her then?"

The man in front of us sucked his mouth to one side. "Kill her," he said, finally. "We can't have any witnesses. And be quick about it. We've got company."

I didn't see it. But I heard it. A gunshot, muffled by the boards in the windows. And, through the gaps, I could see Ginger slump over, blood pooling at her feet.

James was pounding on the boards, screaming over and over, wordless cries of horror.

"Enough!" yelled the man. "You're next."

January's hair had turned bright, furious red and a loop of it shot out, straight towards the man's gun. A shot went off, landing harmlessly in the ground.

"Run!" I bellowed at the top of my lungs. "Guys, get out of here!" In the commotion, I didn't look at Sam and James, but I heard them take off and crash through the bushes. I know this makes me a terrible friend, but I didn't give them too much thought. All my attention was on January.

The man was looming over her, trying to untangle his hand from her hair, trying to shoot again. She was fighting back. Her hair was wrapping itself around his eyes, slipping lower to his neck and then coiling around, twisting itself, tightening. January's face was turning pale with the effort and every breath was coming in quick gasps.

"Leon, run," she panted. "I've got this. It was me they came for anyway."

"I'm not leaving you!" I screamed.

Her eyes were wild. "Go, the other men will be out of that mill and chasing after us at any minute."

I didn't care. I snatched up a rock and smashed it down on the man's head. The way it sounded made me sick to my stomach. I knew I would never forget that dull crack, like the sound a snail's shell makes when you accidentally step on it. He dropped to the ground as I seized January's hand and pulled her into a run. "Make for their van!" I yelled. We jumped inside and January slammed the locks down. The keys were in the ignition and I fumbled with them, forcing them to turn.

The two men who had killed Ginger were bearing down on us, guns aimed at our heads, as the engine roared into life. I slammed my foot on the accelerator and the van lurched back towards the road.

"What about the others?" whispered January.

"They got away," I said. My heart was hammering inside my chest as if it wanted to burst out. "They'll be fine." My tone did not sound convincing.

"Where are we going?" asked January. Her chest was still heaving and her hair was the palest orange I'd ever seen.

"Anywhere as long as it's in the opposite direction to them. Who the hell were those men?"

She closed her eyes. She took so long to reply, I thought she wasn't going to. Then she said: "They're the bad guys. And now they're after us."

ROZ MACLAREN

Chapter Eight

Dogs can run at a speed of between 15–20 miles per hour.

The thing about running is once you start, you can't stop. And the thing about being chased is you're always looking over your shoulder. You're never relaxed. Even when I was twenty miles out of town, I was still driving like a maniac. I couldn't stop replaying the gunshots in my head. They sounded so much louder than I would've expected them to. My ears were still ringing. And worse than that were the pictures that kept flashing into my mind. Images of Ginger. The way she slumped forward, like all the life had gone out of her. *Because it had.* I swallowed hard, trying not to cry. Ginger. We'd grown up together. She and James actually made me believe that true love was a real thing. From the minute he saw her on our first day at school, he was smitten. Sam and I teased him relentlessly about his crush, but James barely noticed, let alone cared. The first time he spoke to her, we were five and at the one plus one equals two stage of our school days. James would probably have carried on loving her from afar, but Sam and I set them up on a date when we got to high school and they'd been inseparable ever since. They were going to be together forever. Probably go to the same college. Probably get married and have kids of their own someday. Ginger couldn't just be dead.

Yet she was. I'd seen her. I'd seen the way those men had killed her as casually as if she was a pesky housefly in their way. My legs couldn't stop shaking, which was making it really hard to change gear effectively. I didn't feel in full control of anything, yet I didn't dare take my foot off the accelerator.

"Slow the hell down," January ordered. "They're not anywhere near."

"And you know this how?" I snapped.

"Because I have working eyes and I can see. We're safe for now. Slow down."

I slowed down. My heart was still hammering. I didn't know where I was going and I was scared. "What did those men mean, when they said Ginger was the wrong girl? Are they after you?"

January shrugged her shoulders sadly. "It's not the first time Mom and I have had to go on the run from people like that."

My eyes widened. I probably looked like some kind of unhinged bush baby. "And you didn't think to mention this before? What are you, a criminal?"

January's voice rose. "No, of course not! Look, I don't know who they are. I don't know what they want. I don't ask questions, I just keep my hat on and my head down and I try to blend in. And I guess somewhere along the line my cover broke and they found me."

"You're telling me armed killers are chasing you and it happens so regularly you don't even ask why?" I spluttered.

January shrugged. "Mom knows. I don't. She won't tell me. Says the less I know the better. I know it sounds crazy."

I let out a sarcastic laugh. "No, we're way past crazy. We were actually past crazy when it turned out you had magic hair."

"Will you stop calling it that!" she demanded. "It's not magic hair, it's just hair! I'm sorry I don't have all the fricking answers, okay?"

"Don't be sorry about that. Be sorry that our friend died and it's your fault." The minute the words were out my mouth, I regretted them. The silence hung, thick and heavy, like a fog between us. I swallowed and reached out. I took her hand. "I'm sorry."

"No." Her voice sounded like she was choking. "It is my fault. I should have told Mom the minute I used my hair on Earwig. But I didn't." She shot me a glance. "Ask me why I didn't."

"Why?"

January's voice cracked. "Because she'd have moved us again. She'd have kept me safe. She'd have kept your friend safe. You wouldn't be on the run with me in a stolen van because my mom is smart and sensible and caring. But I never told her because I couldn't bear to move again. I couldn't bear not knowing you."

I couldn't bear not knowing you.

Have nicer words ever been spoken? I didn't think so.

"I hate moving constantly and not getting attached to people," January was saying. "But she was right. Mom was right. And poor Ginger died because I wanted friends, for the first time in my life."

"January…" I squeezed her hand tightly. "It's not selfish to want a normal life. It's not selfish to want friends. It's not selfish to want to stay in the one place."

January sighed and pressed her cheek to the window. "Do you think the others got away?"

I had been wondering that. "Here," I said, digging in my pockets. "Take my phone. The password is 'password.'"

"So original." January rolled her eyes. "I'm in. What now?"

"Call Sam."

I heard the phone ring out. Once. Twice. Three times. Then Sam answered. "Leon, where the hell are you? Are you okay? Are you alive? Have you been killed?"

"Slow the heck down, Sam, it's January."

"Oh. Well, where the hell is Leon? Is he okay? Is he alive? Has he…"

"He's fine!" interrupted January. "We both are. We wanted to check on you guys." She made it sound so natural, like a casual phone call. Was I the only one freaking out that we'd just barely made it away from those killers?

Sam's voice crackled distantly. "Yeah, we're the police station now. James is in giving them a statement."

"Did Ginger make it?"

There was a pause. "She bled out. She died before the ambulance got to her."

January's eyes closed. She was squeezing the phone so tightly, her fingers were turning white. "Tell James I'm so sorry," she whispered.

"Are you guys coming back? The police are looking for the killers. You should be safe…" January ended the call, cutting Sam's words off.

"What the hell?" I demanded. "Why did you hang up?"

"Because there is no safe anymore," January snapped. "And I'm not dragging anyone else into danger with me. Stop the van."

I slammed on the brakes. She tried to open the door, but the locks were still on and she ineffectually wrenched the handle for a few minutes before pausing to slam her fist on the dashboard three times.

"Finished?" I asked, lifting an eyebrow.

"This isn't a joke." She turned to me. "You need to go home. Those men are after me. And you have to leave or they'll kill you. I can't make it any clearer than that."

"Well, I'm going to make this clear." I picked up both her hands. "We're in this together. We're friends, you and me. And I don't abandon my friends."

January rolled her eyes. That was slightly hurtful, considering I was putting my life on the line for her. I'd hoped the shared trauma might bring us closer together, the way it always does in the movies. "You need to cut the hero act. You need to think of yourself. You are going to die if you come with me."

I shook my head. "Neither of us are going to die. We are going to find out what these men want and where they came from and we are going to think of a plan. Together. Okay?"

I expected her to protest and argue with me. But the fight had gone out of her. She just smiled weakly at me and said: "It's your funeral, kid." But she squeezed my hand. I think that was her way of saying thank you.

My phone buzzed with a notification and I checked it, hoping it was from Sam.

It wasn't. A news app I used was alerting me to the fact that a video, posted yesterday, had gone viral. This wouldn't normally be noteworthy, but the video was filmed in my town. So far, it had racked up five million views.

Out of curiosity, I clicked on it and my heart sank.

"January."

"What?" She was twisting a strand of orange hair around her fingertip. The color of her hair told me she was still scared. The viral video in front of me told me she had reason to be.

ROZ MACLAREN

Chapter Nine

Cuddling someone you love help you recover quicker if you're unwell.

"January…" I repeated.

"Yeah?"

"You asked how they knew where you were." I handed her the phone. "This is how."

GIRL BRUTALLY ATTACKS—WITH HER HAIR?!?!

As titles go, I think Karen could have come up with better. Then again, it went viral so she must have done something right. Brooke Cox had obviously been filming while all our eyes were on January. The footage was shaky and grainy, but unmistakably January.

The description read: "Meet January Hill, the newest student at the Hamilton Institute, a high school in one of the state's sleepiest little villages. Just don't get too close to her. As the film shows, she's dangerous."

January let out a stream of curse words, calling Karen all manner of horrible names. I gently took my phone back. The video had been shared three million times and had over ten and a half million comments. Most of them seemed to think the whole thing was staged.

CoolGuy: Soooooo fake.

ElectricEel: I can literally see the strings you used to manipulate her hair here. How stupid do you think people are?

BlowUrMind: U probably deserved it.

The comments were all of a similar ilk, ranging from disbelieving to insulting. But one of them made my heart beat faster. One of them made my tongue feel so dry, I thought it was going to permanently stick itself to the roof of my mouth.

AprilShowers: My hair does this too.
My hair does this too.

"January." I nudged her. "January, look."

"What? Has yet another aspect of my life been ruined?" She took the phone and blinked at the screen. "Wow. Think she's for real?"

I shrugged and tapped her username. "She's called April Tyler." I did a quick search for her on the various socials. She was surprisingly easy to find. The first result had the same profile picture as the AprilShowers account. I scrolled through pictures of a teenage girl, wearing a sun hat, laughing with friends, playing with a dog that looked more like a bear. Her location was posted for all to see. A town called Lighthampton. I wondered if she knew just what danger she might have put herself in. If they had come for January, would they go for her?

"I didn't know there was anyone else like me," January said. "Not to sound like I'm blowing my own horn, you know. But yeah. Never met anyone who could do what I can with my hair. She's probably lying. Just attention-seeking."

A growing wave of dread washed over me. "And if she's not? What if the same people who are looking for you look for her too? She's sixteen."

"That's literally the same age as us. Plus she's got a family." January stabbed her finger at a photograph of April being simultaneously embraced by a man and woman, presumably her parents. "They can look after her."

I sighed, dragging a hand through my hair. "I think we should…"

"Don't say it."

"…Go and find her."

"I knew you were going to say that!" exclaimed

January. "We can barely take care of ourselves, let alone look after someone else."

"Then do what you want!" I snapped. "Go and look after number one, like you always do. But I'm not standing by while another kid gets shot, just like Ginger. Not on my watch. And if you're not coming, you'd better get the hell out of here because this van is going to Lighthampton."

January glared at me. She folded her arms. "Fine, then," she muttered. "Go and play the hero. See where it gets you." When I didn't respond, she said: "We don't even know anyone in Lighthampton."

I hesitated. "Actually, we do."

****

He never said he was leaving.

He never said he had met someone else.

He never said he hated us, but he must have because why else would he leave?

Mom had a bit of a breakdown after he left. Actually, that's putting it mildly. She had a *lot* of a breakdown. She tried to put a brave face on and smile and say she didn't need a man anyway but she stopped showering, stopped working, stopped eating. Just stopped. It was like Dad had stopped time and she was frozen.

I tried to cook. To this day, I can make a mean spaghetti on toast. I tried to hold what was left of my family together. But it seemed pointless. Dad hadn't thought our family was worth holding together. Maybe he was right.

Mom lost her job. That tends to happen if you don't show up after a couple of weeks. People make allowances at first, but, eventually, they have to draw the line.

She got the letter about a month after Dad left.

She left it, with all the other letters, in a pile on the mat. I had to open it. I had to read the news that she was no longer part of the team at Tatler & Bosworth Accountants.

I got a weekend job at the supermarket. Eight dollars an hour and a staff discount. It paid for our food, our electricity, our rent. Just.

I sold the television and the dishwasher. Mom threw a fit. The television was all she lived for. Maybe the reality shows made her feel she had her own life under control. After all, when the headline is "I'm addicted to [redacted] with my [insert close family relative's name here] while my best friend watches" then your own life looks a bit more normal. Even if an accurate summary of that life would be "My husband left me and I haven't showered in three weeks."

It took Mom two years to get herself together. I managed to get her a job at the supermarket. She eventually worked her way up to manager. I didn't quite know how, since she was hopeless at managing her own life. But she put on a good show at work. To the outside world, I guess she looked like any other single mother.

I wondered if she would even notice that I'd gone missing. I wondered if she'd even care.

Thinking about all the stuff Mom did made me wonder something else. What if Dad wasn't the bad guy? What if he'd just had enough?

Chapter Ten

About 1.5 million kids run away each year.

I remember reading about runaway teenagers when I was about thirteen, waiting in the doctor's surgery to pick up Mom's prescription. That's probably where I remembered that statistic from, though it could well be out of date now. There were all sorts of leaflets, mainly dealing with what to do if you're pregnant for the first time, how to handle bullying, or if you're contemplating running away from home. I was unlikely to get pregnant and I figured there wasn't much a leaflet could do to stop me being bullied, so I picked up the leaflet about runaways and started reading.

The leaflet said most kids leave because of trouble at home. It did not, however, comment on what to do if you're running away because bad guys want to abduct your friend because she has magical hair.

I guessed that was something I'd have to find out for myself.

I think I know why I was so obsessed with facts at that age. They distracted me from the bigger picture, from the fact that my life was spiraling out of my control. They'd done it then and they were doing it now. Because the real question I should have been asking as I drove the van to Lighthampton was: "What the hell am I going to say to my father?"

It was four years since he left us and two years since I last saw him. Memories of that excruciating meeting floated back into my mind as I absentmindedly drove along.

Some fast food place. Lunch hour. I don't know who picked that or why it felt like a good idea to go at its busiest time. Jostled by school kids in black pants and white shirts. Spotty boys, their hair shiny and spiky with gel, trying to chat up pretty girls who looked like they'd never had a hamburger in their lives. Young moms and dads with screaming, projectile-vomiting kids trailing coloring books, pens, and toys behind them, and arguing with each other about whether a burger had too many calories for their little darling to handle.

"You okay, son?" Dad had asked. "This place used to be your favorite."

Yeah, when I was seven. "Favorites change," I muttered.

"Kids, eh?" Dad glanced around at his new wife and his old one. "I can't keep up with what's in and what's not, these days."

Suzanne kept jiggling her leg, up and down. Cleo wasn't born then, but Meredith was there. "I hate the food here," she groaned, although she ate a double cheeseburger, all her chips, all my chips, and most of Suzanne's.

"How about we go for a walk?" Suzanne suggested. "Let you and Leon catch up."

"No, stay." My dad put his hand on her knee. "We're all family now. We can all catch up together. Get to know each other. Right, Leon?"

"We're all family?" echoed my mother. "Are you actually serious?"

"Megan, please," my dad groaned. "Let's not do this now, please?"

"I'm just at a total loss how you expect me to be family with her." My mother pointed at Suzanne. "Am I actually supposed to be family with your bit on the side?"

"She's my wife, Megan, whether you like it or not, and…"

It was starting again. So I got up. I took my tray over to the cleaning station. I carefully dumped the empty cartons my burger and chips had come in. My fingers were shaking while I scraped tomato ketchup–coated fries into the bin. I could feel everyone watching me as I walked out the door.

That was the last time I saw my dad. He called occasionally. Wrote even less frequently. Suggested meeting up once or twice, but I always had an excuse and he eventually gave up asking. We drifted out of contact and got on with our lives. Going by his social media, his life was happier now I wasn't in it.

And there I was, driving up to his door, ready to disrupt his perfect little life all over again.

****

The two-story red brick apartment wasn't that scary, and yet my palms were sweating and my heart felt like it was going to jump out of my chest and run away down the street. It was strange. I'd wanted this for ages. I'd wanted to go and see my dad. And now that I was actually on his doorstep, I was inches from turning away and never coming back. In fact, I probably would have done just that, if it weren't for the girl standing next to me.

January slipped her hand into mine. She was the one who rang the bell. She was the one who knocked loudly when nobody answered. And she was the one who tried the door handle, swung the door open and yelled: "Anyone home?"

A child toddled into view, wearing only a diaper and trailing a one-eyed bear after itself. It blinked at us with big blue eyes. My eyes.

"That's Cleo," I said. "My dad's new kid."

"Your sister." January stared, wide-eyed.

"Half-sister," I corrected.

Suzanne appeared, juggling a milk bottle and a carton of yogurt, a phone sandwiched between her ear and her shoulder. When she saw me, she dropped the phone and stood, staring at me. "Leon?" she whispered.

"Um, hi, Suzanne. Is Dad around?"

"He's out at work, but I'll call him. I'm sure he'll be able to take the rest of the day off. I'll call him," she babbled.

January, meanwhile, had swooped down and lifted Cleo off her feet and was embracing the rather sticky toddler. "I just love kids," she confessed, looking at a bewildered Suzanne. "This one's sweet."

Suzanne still looked as though someone had just told her we were about to be invaded by aliens. "Um. Let me call Mike."

"Sure. Thanks." January smiled at her, as naturally as if she talked to her friend's estranged father's wife every day of her life. "Me and Leon will take this little cutie into the living room while you call Mike. Thanks!"

We left Suzanne blinking and wandered into the living room. It was strewn with toys, so we treaded carefully and found a safe path to the couch. The walls were filled with pictures—happy family pictures, photographs of sunsets, dogs, horses, beaches. Everything felt happy, even if it was messy.

"She seemed nice," January whispered, jiggling Cleo up and down on her knee.

"Do you actually like kids?" I whispered back.

"Sure." January ruffled Cleo's hair.

"January, I think this whole thing was a bad idea. I think…"

Suzanne came back in. "He's coming home." She sat down opposite us and smiled. "It's good to see you. And Cleo has certainly taken a shine to you…" She paused, looking at January.

"This is Jane," I said, quickly. "Jane Paterson. She's a friend from school."

Suzanne nodded. "Right…" She leaned forward. "Look, Leon. I'm not stupid."

"What?" I blustered.

"You've not spoken to your dad much in the past few years, and now you're suddenly here. Which is totally fine, by the way. I just … I need to know if you're in trouble." She looked at me, so kindly, so desperate to be friends that I had to look at the ceiling rather quickly in case she saw my eyes getting misty.

"We're fine," January lied, smoothly. "School just broke up and we thought we'd visit a friend of mine in the area. Leon didn't want to come so close and not see his dad, so we spontaneously popped in. No one's in trouble."

Suzanne's shoulders relaxed. "Okay then," she smiled. "Who's your friend? Maybe I know them?"

January hesitated, just for a second. Her first mistake. She glanced at me and I said the first name that came into my mind. "April Tyler."

Suzanne's face turned white. "Oh, wow. Um. I don't know how to say this. April… She's been reported missing."

ROZ MACLAREN

Chapter Eleven

It is possible to be frightened to death. During terrifying moments, calcium is injected into the heart cells. If the threat is too scary, the brain doesn't know when to stop with the calcium and the person can die.

Let's just say January and I probably had an overdose of calcium in our hearts right about then.

January recovered first. "We need to go." She tugged my hand urgently and attempted to put little Cleo on the ground. Cleo did not take kindly to this and clung on with the strength of a thousand ivy plants.

"Go?" Suzanne's eyebrows shot up. "But what about…"

I heard the front door click. "Hello!"

My dad walked in.

I've rewritten that sentence a thousand times. I've tried to explain how I felt, how my palms suddenly produced enough sweat to cover my entire body, how my tongue went as dry as a cactus and my calcium-filled heart started beating overtime.

It all sounds so made up, like those cringy, slow-motion scenes in films where the main characters just stare at each other.

I couldn't meet his eyes, but I knew he was looking at me. I could feel his gaze moving over me. "Leon…"

"Hi, Dad." *Keep it casual, Leon. Play it cool.*

He strode over and patted me gently on the shoulder. "Good to see you, son. Does your mother know you're here?" He glanced edgily over his shoulder, as if she was concealed in a cupboard waiting to jump out and shout at him for choosing Suzanne over her.

"Hi." January pumped his hand up and down in a

forceful shake. "I'm Jan…"

"Jane." I shot her a glance. "Jane Paterson, my friend from school."

January gave me a small nod of approval. Even I didn't know how I'd remembered to call her by her fake name. How I'd not blown our cover. Maybe when your life is falling apart, it makes you remember the little things. Like random trivia that means nothing in the grand scheme of things.

Although there was no random trivia in my head just at that moment. All I could think of was that my dad, who I hadn't seen in two years, was standing right in front of me, looking as awkward as … well, me at a school dance.

"I'm really sorry we have to cut and run," January was saying. "We've had some bad news."

My dad took it all very calmly. "That's fine," he said, smoothly. "You won't mind if I call Megan just to let her know you got here safely."

He knew. He *so* knew. And the look of horror January shot me just confirmed his suspicions.

"Okay, what's going on?" Dad was using his Extra Stern Dad voice on me. I hadn't heard it in years. Was it weird to realize that I'd actually missed it?

I really wanted to tell him. I really wanted someone to listen and then say: "Right, I know exactly what to do. Leave it to me." I wanted my dad to be the hero of this story.

But I couldn't tell him. Somewhere, out there, were men willing to kill schoolgirls. They wouldn't hesitate to shoot my dad and I couldn't let that happen.

I called his bluff. "Sure, call her," I said. "But we really have to run. I'll come back. I'll explain." I was backing out the door.

Say something, I was telepathically begging my

dad. *Say something, anything, make me turn around, tell me I have to stop, ground me if you have to. Just don't let me go like this because if you do I'll know you never really cared about me.*

He let me go. He never said a word, just watched as I walked out of his house.

We were back out in the warm air, just January and me and a stolen van and no idea what to do next.

Well, getting in the van seemed like an obvious move, so we both did that. I pulled out my phone and searched "April Tyler disappearance." Hits. Too many hits. Major news sites covering April's disappearance.

"The bad guys got to her." April, with her sunny smile and her big dog and her YouTube account. I pictured her, terrified and screaming as they took her. I pictured her dead, like Ginger.

I'm not the hero in this story. Heroes don't turn to the girl next to them, the girl with scared, orange hair, and say: "What do we do?"

Maybe January is the hero. Because she knew exactly what to do.

****

"Hi, Mrs. Tyler?"

Pale face, big eyes, no makeup. Hard to tell what she might have looked like if she hadn't been peering through a barely open door.

"I don't want to talk to any journalists. I can't." Her voice had the clogged sound people get when they've been crying a lot. My mom's voice was similar after Dad left.

"Tell them to go away, Mary!" yelled a man's voice from the background.

"I'm trying!"

"Mrs. Tyler?" January's voice was smooth. "We're not journalists. We're not police. We're the people who know who took your daughter."

Three sentences. One of them absolutely guaranteed to make Mrs. Tyler open up, invite us in and give us tea. Yep, January's your hero here. I'm just along for the ride.

"Tell me." As soon as we were inside, Mrs. Tyler leaned forward, grabbing January's shoulders. "For goodness' sake, tell me. The police are saying April just ran away. Like me and Jamie are bad to her somehow. We're not. April's a good girl, she's a happy girl." Mrs. Tyler couldn't choke the sob back and I had to stare hard at the ceiling. (It was a hideous 1970s-style one with yucky textured swirls.) The enormous Newfoundland dog that April had been cuddling in her social media photographs padded in and put its giant head on my knee. It looked at me with soulful brown eyes and I wondered if it was missing April too.

"When did she go missing?" January asked.

Mrs. Tyler let out a shaky sigh. "Yesterday. She just didn't come home from school. Vanished. She means the absolute world to us. Me and Jamie weren't able to have children, so we adopted April when she was a baby."

I saw something change in January's face. The briefest of frowns. She didn't let her mask slip for long, though. "And, up until then, you hadn't seen anyone hanging around. No suspicious-looking men?"

"No, everything was normal." Mrs. Tyler's voice broke with a sound of desperation and anguish. "Please tell me. Where did she go? You said you knew."

"Tell me, Mrs. Tyler…" January paused, presumably for dramatic effect. Like there wasn't already enough drama. "Could April do this?" She took a deep breath and I stared as her now-purple hair lifted and waved cheerily at Mrs. Tyler.

Chapter Twelve

Sunflowers can help clean radioactive soil.
There was nothing relevant about that fact. I just like the image of hundreds of sunflowers, facing the sun in defiance, refusing to die because of radiation.
Focus, Leon. Pay attention.
"How did you know?" Mrs. Tyler's voice had changed. "April hardly spoke about it. She was shy, to be honest. We encouraged that. Didn't want the kids at school to tease her. You know how it can be."

Neither January or I wanted to tell her that April's biggest worry was no longer school bullies.

"April got careless," January said. "She revealed this information on a viral video. We think that's linked to her disappearance."

"And you need to tell the police this," I interrupted. "Fast."

Mrs. Tyler looked even more anguished. "Who on earth would believe me? My daughter had special powers and that's why she was taken? They'd take me next … to the hospital."

January's hair was turning orange again. She was getting scared. "Mrs. Tyler, where did you adopt April from?"

"A shelter near here. They found April in an airport. Someone had put her in a suitcase and it ended up finding its way on a plane to the city. It was a paperwork nightmare for the shelter, to be honest. April came from up north and, from what I understand, it was a headache trying to sort it all out. Anyway, nobody claimed her and we felt so sorry for her, we took her."

I looked at Mary Tyler's face. Her eyes whispered of a totally sleepless night, of a woman who was fearing the worst for the child she loved. They were the kind, decent eyes of an ordinary person in an extraordinary mess. Of someone who was refusing to give in. Maybe that sunflower fact wasn't so random after all. Maybe Mary Tyler was a sunflower.

Maybe I could be too.

Mrs. Tyler was still talking. "We always told her if ever she wanted to find her birth parents, she could. I think that's what the police think happened. That she's just taken off to try and find them."

"And you think otherwise?" asked January.

Mrs. Tyler folded her arms defensively. "Yes. April would talk to me. She would talk to Jamie. I know that for a fact. If she wanted to find her birth parents, she knows we'd do everything we could to make that happen for her."

There was something so honest about her face. And something so broken.

I realized then why I felt so protective of her. Her face had the same expression my mom's did when my dad left. Devastation doesn't even begin to cover it.

I had tried to look after Mom. I had failed.

Maybe I could do better for Mary Tyler.

"We need to leave," I heard myself say. "Tell the police, if they'll listen to you, Mrs. Tyler. But my friend and I are going to try and find April."

January turned to stare at me. "We're going to what?"

"Not now." I silenced her with a glance. "Mrs. Tyler, one more thing. Why did you call her April?"

Mrs. Tyler half-smiled. "I didn't. Not really. It was tattooed on the back of her neck."

I frowned. "What was?"

"The name. April. I thought it was terrible. I mean, who tattoos a baby? But the name … it stuck. It suited her. So we kept it."

I forget what we said next or how we ended up outside, but as soon as we were back in the van, I grabbed January, lifted her hair, and looked at the back of her neck.

I didn't want to see it, but it was there. Tattooed in small but distinctive writing.

"January."

It was the first time I'd ever touched her hair. It didn't feel like anyone else's. It felt like hundreds of tiny live wires, sparking with energy, alive with electricity.

Her hair was pushing my hand away. "Leave me alone."

"Why didn't you tell me you had a tattoo?" I asked, although it was a stupid question.

January knew that. January pounced. "Oh, what, I'm going to rock up on my first day at school. Hi, Leon. By the way, I've got a tattoo."

I folded my arms. "A tattoo you've had since you were a baby! A tattoo identical to another girl's, a girl who also happens to have magic hair?"

"Not quite identical. Hers says April. Mine says January." She tried for a sassy smile. She failed.

"And you both just happen to be named after months of the year? January, what the hell is going on?"

"How should I know? Up until recently, I thought I was the only one like this! Now there are two of me!"

"And you're both from the Northeast." So many puzzle pieces. No clue what any of them meant. I wanted to scream in frustration.

"Maybe we're sisters. I have no idea." January's hair spilled over her shoulders, almost as if it was trying to hug her. It was slowly turning black. I didn't know what that meant about her mood and I didn't like to ask.

"We need to go," she was saying. "We can't just sit here. Mrs. Tyler is still watching us from the window,

I'm pretty sure. I wish we'd never come here. We just made it worse."

"We did our best. We've given them the best chance of finding April alive." I pulled slowly out of the driveway.

"They won't find her alive. They want to kill her and kill me. They'll find her body. They're too late to find her. Then they'll probably find our bodies too." She took my hand. "It's not too late. You can go home. Go back to your dad. Stay alive."

I shook her hand off. "We're in this together," I growled. "And we're going to find that kid and she's going to be alive."

"Saying it doesn't make it so."

"January."

"What?"

"What the hell are you?" She blinked at me, not understanding, so I threw some options at her. "A robot? An experiment? An alien?"

She looked at me, almost sadly. "I'm just a teenage girl trying to get through high school. Other than that? I have absolutely no idea."

She didn't know it then, but she was a sunflower.

Chapter Thirteen

Anything is possible on the dark web.

Not really a fact—more something Sam told me when I called him. I was hoping he would tell me what to do, not direct me to the scary corners of the Internet.

"The dark web?" I repeated. "Seriously?"

"Seriously. I can find out why there are two girls of a similar age with similar tattoos, but I'll need to go on the dark web to do it."

"Sammy…"

"Trust me. I've got your back. I'll find out what's going on and I'll find a way to stop it." He sounded so confident. I couldn't figure out if he was faking it for my benefit.

"How long will it take?"

"I'm already on it." I could hear his fingers running over a keyboard.

****

In books, when people run away, they never get cold or hungry or tired or irritable. January and I were all of those things. I also *really* wanted a shower. My hair was turning greasy and my body was sticky with sweat from all the running and stressing. I had been driving for three hours, not sure whether I was going north or south and not sure if I really cared. I figured if we kept moving, the men would have less chance of finding us.

"We need to stop," January said. "We've been going nonstop for hours. I'm tired and I'm hungry."

"What am I supposed to do?" I snapped. "Do you want me to pull over and paint a big red arrow on the road pointing at us so the bad guys know where we are?"

January's hair turned red. "No, I just want some food, is that a crime?"

I slammed on the brakes and pulled over. "Here

we go. I've stopped."

It was dark, but we both knew we were in the middle of nowhere. Food was looking more and more unlikely.

"Look," I said, apologetically. "I'm sorry. I just don't know what to do and I want to keep us both safe. How about we try and get some sleep for now and see what happens in the morning? You go and take the back of the van and I'll sleep across the seats here."

January nodded abruptly. She got out and I heard the rear doors open and then close. I sighed and snuggled down into my hoodie, ready to go to sleep when someone rapped on the van window. I nearly jumped out of my skin until I realized it was January.

"What the hell?" I demanded.

"You need to see this."

I followed her round to the back of the van, and, when she opened the doors, my jaw dropped in shock.

Guns. Lots and lots of guns.

Food. Lots and lots of food.

"Oh, thank God," I breathed. "Now maybe you'll finally shut up about being hungry."

We shut ourselves in the back of the van, locking every door, and began a feast. Cold meat and tinned fish doesn't sound all that exciting—unless you haven't eaten for a solid ten hours.

"Can you shoot a gun?" January asked me, through a mouthful of ham.

"Yeah," I replied, in between gulping down orange juice. "I can." It was one of the few things my dad had taught me before he left. We used to line up tin cans in the back garden. He taught me how to hold the gun, how to squeeze the trigger, and how to shoot straight.

I didn't tell January that I hadn't fired a gun once in the past four years. Or that my only real experience was with an air rifle.

January was making up a bed out of blankets and cushions. "Whoever these men are, they were planning on staying here for some time," she remarked. "There's weapons enough for an entire army—and food enough for about a year." She finished patting her cushions into place and I figured that was my cue to leave. "Where are you going?" she asked, as I scrambled across the van.

"To leave you in peace to sleep," I replied.

She blinked in surprise. "You don't have to. There's enough room here for both of us."

I looked at the makeshift bed. "You sure?"

"Leon." She looked at me in a way that indicated she thought I had the mental intellect of a cabbage. "We're hiding in God knows where pursued by armed men who want to kill us both. That rather outweighs the risk of you suddenly ravishing me in the back of a van, don't you think?"

I laughed and snuggled down into the blankets. No bed had ever felt as good before. "If I was going to ravish you, I wouldn't do it in the back of a van," I said, trying for a jokey and flirtatious tone.

"No? Where then?" She got in beside me, without a hint of shyness. Her hair splayed across the cushions, and it was pale blue—like the sea on a moonlit night.

"I wouldn't ravish you at all," I said, softly. The mood in the van had suddenly shifted and I was serious. "I wish things could have been different, as I think we could have been good friends at the very least, but with all this crap going on, you've got enough to deal with."

January's eyes widened a little, as if she hadn't been expecting that reply. Then she did something I would never have expected in a million years.

She leaned over, closed the gap between us and kissed me.

That's right. I had my first kiss in the back of a stolen van, where armed killers could break in and shoot us at any moment.

I cupped my hands around her cheeks and kissed her back, softly at first. Not one of those heavy-duty make out sessions you see in films. This was gentle. This was sweet. She tasted like bubblegum and hope and sadness and I never wanted it to end. I'd probably still be there kissing her if my phone hadn't rung at that exact minute.

It's quite hard to keep a romantic atmosphere when you've got the heavy metal opening of a 1970s rock song blaring right in your ear. (Note to self: change ring tone and sue the band for interrupting my first kiss.)

I glanced at my phone. Sam. I thought seriously about killing him the next time I saw him. "Hey, Sam," I answered the phone, trying to sound nonchalant and not at all like someone who has just had their first kiss.

"Leon. Me and James have been doing some digging. Not a lot came up first time around, but I found something that might be interesting."

"Spill."

"Around sixteen years ago, twelve babies were pronounced stillborn in a hospital up in Inverhamilton. All of the babies were girls and all of them 'died' within the same month."

"I don't get it," I said, disappointment leaking into my voice. "What's that got to do with anything?"

"They were the only ones."

"What?"

"They were the only ones stillborn that month. And there were twelve of them!"

I still didn't get it. Sam, being the good friend that he is, knew from my telling silence that I didn't get it.

"How many months of the year are there?" he

asked, with exaggerated patience.

I glanced at January, her face still inches away from mine. "Twelve," I said. "There are twelve of them." *January and April. Two months of the year. Two tattoos, to tell them apart.*

Sam's voice was still crackling in my ear. His words made my skin turn to gooseflesh. "So I'm saying they didn't die at all. I'm saying they were stolen. And I'm saying they were used for something. Something bad."

ROZ MACLAREN

Chapter Fourteen

A kiss stimulates twenty-nine muscles and chemicals to facilitate relaxation.

So, really, I was doing January a favor by kissing her so often.

And Sam was definitely *not* doing me a favor by interrupting me every time.

It was a text this time, and not a phone call. All the same, I pulled away from January reluctantly and said: "I'd better check it."

Sam: **Jess Hill is missing.**

Sam was never one for being overly verbose but, on this occasion, I think his text could have been improved by more information. Although he sent just enough to make my heart skip a beat.

"What's wrong?" asked January, chewing her bottom lip, which, moments ago, I had been kissing.

I hesitated, unsure how to tell her. I decided to do a Sam and go for the jugular. "Your mom's missing."

"What?" She snatched the phone and read the message for herself.

I called Sam. "Hey."

"Hi," he crackled into my ear. "How are you?"

"Still alive. Do you know when Jess went missing?"

"Nope. We may have slightly broken into the house."

"You did what?" I demanded.

"Had to, man. The cat was still there and he was hungry. Now, I don't know about you, but I know people like Jess never go away and leave their cat hungry. So I took him home and he's with me now."

"That's very compassionate, Sam, but a woman is

missing here."

"Well, missing is a bit of a stretch. I mean, we tried reporting it to the police but they didn't want to know. Apparently when you're over eighteen you can go missing and nobody will bat an eyelid. They just said she moves around a lot anyway and maybe she just decided to move on. I call bull, considering her house is still fully furnished. Not to mention the whole cat thing."

"Sammy…" Did I say he was a boy of few words? I lied. I was struggling to get a word in edgewise.

Sam was still talking. "I'm thinking maybe the bad guys got her or maybe she went to look for January. Either way, we have no way of knowing. Oh, and your mom thinks you're staying at mine, by the way. She called asking if I knew where you were and I told her you were with me."

"Wow, I'm surprised she even noticed I left the house."

"I know you're doing the whole dramatic runaway thing and protecting the innocent young maiden, but have you thought where this is going to end?"

My mouth went dry. "What do you mean?"

"Like, if these bad guys can organize a hospital cover-up and steal twelve babies, then they're powerful. You can run, but they'll always be behind you. I'm saying: this isn't going to go away. We need backup."

Timing. Split second, perfect timing. It can mean the difference between life and death. And Sam's timing was spot on. Because, seconds after he said that, shots were fired and bullet holes appeared in the van doors. Moonlight streamed in, like miniature spotlights.

"Sam, I gotta go!" I threw myself over the chairs and into the van cab, fumbling with the keys. Why is it nothing ever works when it needs to? The van coughed, sounding apologetic. "Come on, baby," I muttered. "Turn over."

January climbed over the seats to join me, just as the engine roared into life and we shot forward. She had two guns on her knee.

"Are they loaded?" I demanded, as I spun the wheel round. Gunshots roared in my ears.

January pointed the gun out the window and squeezed the trigger. Glass shattered and cold air rushed in. "Yep."

"Goodness' sake, January!"

The men fired back and I felt the van's height drop. The steering wheel wrenched itself out of my hand and we were spinning, sliding, slipping out of control.

Trees came closer and closer, and I threw myself over January, knocking her down to the floor. The impact came, knocking the breath out of our bodies and the wind out of our lungs.

Footsteps. Echoing through the quiet of the night.

I picked up January's gun and waited. Our breathing sounded so incredibly loud. Another shot and the windscreen shattered down on top of us in a rain of broken glass.

"Stay down," January whispered.

"January, wait, what the hell are you doing?" I hissed as she slowly rose to her feet and forced open the van door.

"It's me you want," I heard her clear voice say. "Go ahead and get this over with."

I crouched behind the window. My fingers were shaking as they curved around the gun. I could only see two men. There were probably more. My heart was hammering so loudly I was certain they would hear it.

"Go on then," repeated January. "What the hell are you waiting for? You've chased me halfway across the country. Just kill me and get it done already."

Two of the men advanced on January, guns in hand. My heart drummed inside my chest. I had to do something.

Before I could move, a woman's voice rang out and someone ran into view. "Get the hell away from my daughter!"

"Mom?" January's jaw dropped.

I saw my chance. I stood up and I squeezed the trigger, praying I didn't miss. One man fell to his knees and the other reacted fast, turning to fire a deluge of bullets at me. I ducked behind the van, my heart hammering in my chest.

"Get the hell away from my son!" Another voice pierced the darkness and a familiar figure appeared.

"Dad?" I choked.

I knew it was stupid, but the second I heard his voice, this wave of relief crashed over me. Like, yeah, sure, we might have had two men with guns wanting us dead, but my dad had just showed up so everything was going to be okay.

Except it wasn't. The second man whipped round to aim at my dad. A shot rang through the darkness, so loud it made my ears scream in protest.

Smoke rose from my gun. My fingers were still squeezing the trigger in some kind of death grip. And the man who had been seconds away from killing my dad was on the ground now. I had killed him. I had killed them both. My breathing was coming in desperate chokes and I couldn't stop shaking. Dad walked over to me and put his arm round my shoulder. "Well, son, I see you can still sink a tin can at fifty paces."

I burst into hysterical laughter.

Chapter Fifteen

"The sixth sick sheik's sixth sheep's sick" is said *to be the hardest tongue twister in the English language.*

"Dad?" I repeated. "What are you doing here?"

Dad clapped a hand on my shoulder. "I may not have been around all the time, but I know when something is up, and something was definitely up with you."

"Yeah, but how did you find me?" I demanded.

Dad just smiled, darkly. "I have my ways."

"And how did you find me?" January demanded of her mom.

Our parents ignored us. "Hi." Dad stuck out his hand. "Mike Marsh. Leon's dad."

"Jess Hill. January's mom."

"Um, excuse me, this is a very touching introduction, but some guys just tried to kill us," January said. "And there could be more of them."

"She's right—we should get out of here," agreed Dad. "Leave your car here," he said to January's mom. "We'll take mine. Those guys won't recognize it, but they might know yours."

"No way, not until you tell us what the hell is going on!" I hadn't meant to scream, but going by the shocked faces, I think I did. Can you blame me? My hands were still shaking. I'd just shot and presumably killed two guys. I could see their dark hulks lying on the ground, with a pool of congealing blood leaking onto the ground. Suddenly, that cold meat I'd eaten earlier came rushing to the surface.

Attractive, Leon. Throwing up in front of the girl you like. She's really going to be impressed.

I couldn't look her in the eye, but she walked over to me and took my hand. Something about the gesture made me feel better. Like we were a team. Us against the world. And, so far, it was 1–0 to us.

****

When had it happened? When did my dad transform from average guy into a badass hero? How was he taking all this so calmly? He'd bundled us into his car and he was driving us somewhere safe, all without seeming the slightest bit perturbed.

Then, again, I'd just shot and killed two men and I think I was being pretty calm about that. If you ignore the fact that I was still crying.

January wouldn't have cried. She was already adapting to her new circumstances. "Plan. We need a plan."

"My plan is getting you two kids to safety," Dad said, firmly.

"You don't understand." The desperation in Jess' voice made goosebumps rise on my skin. "There is no safety."

Dad frowned. "Of course there is. We call the police, explain what happened…"

Jess was shaking her head. "No. The police won't help."

I watched Dad's brow furrow even more. "What do you mean?"

"I mean this isn't my first rodeo with these guys, okay?" Jess snapped.

"Mom?" January's voice shook. "Who am I? Where did I come from? Who are they? Why do they want me dead?"

Jess buried her face in her hands. When she lifted her head, she looked to have aged ten years. "Now isn't the time for this."

"Bull!" roared January. "You're stalling because you're too much of a coward to tell me, aren't you? I could die any minute and I won't ever know why unless you tell me. Whatever it is, it can't be any worse than what I'm imagining, so go ahead. Tell me."

My dad shot me the look of a man who was now in way over his head and didn't have a clue what was going on. I shrugged at him. I'd felt that way ever since I met January. Maybe that was partly why I liked her so much.

Jess sighed and raked a hand through her hair. "I don't know who your birth parents are, but I do know you were one of The Twelve."

"The Twelve what? Disciples?"

Jess frowned. "Don't be irreverent. This was sixteen years ago. I worked for an organization up in the Northeast. They were involved in all kinds of secret research. Biological weapons. Cloning. Genetic enhancement. All of the above. It was good money. And I'd just been promoted. Head of a top secret genetic enhancement project. Essentially, it boiled down to turning children into weapons. But, to do that, we needed children."

"The twelve babies from the hospital," I breathed, remembering what Sam had told me.

"Correct." Jess nodded in my direction. "I was told their parents had consented to the experiments. I was in charge of overseeing the genetic enhancement of these twelve babies. It wasn't until later I found out we'd all been lied to." Jess twisted her fingers together, looking down at her hands. "Their parents believed their children had died at birth. And I believed I was doing the right thing."

"When you say genetic enhancement…" I reached over and touched January's hair. It curled round my finger, almost in an affectionate caress. "Did you do this?" I looked at Jess.

She shook her head. "Not me personally, no, but I watched it get done. And other babies got other enhancements. Because there were twelve of them, we named them after months of the year. It seemed more humane than giving them numbers."

January snorted in disdain. "So you'll steal babies from their families without a second thought, but God forbid you give them numbers."

"What happened to the other babies?" I asked.

Jess bit her lip until a bead of red appeared. "I let them go."

"How?" demanded January.

"You were all just kids. And we were experimenting on you like lab rats. Five of the babies were too weak to cope and they died. I was so caught up in telling myself it was for the greater good, but that didn't help me sleep any better at night. I swore I'd do something, even if it killed me—and I knew it might. The man who ran the whole affair … at first I believed everything he said. I overlooked all the things he did that I didn't agree with until I couldn't ignore it all anymore. I knew he'd kill me without a second thought if he thought I was the reason his latest specimens had vanished. But I had to do something. I smuggled the seven survivors out of the lab and I disposed of them."

"Disposed of us?" echoed January. "What, like garbage?"

"No, of course not!" Jess caught hold of January's hand. "I had to get you all to safety. I dropped one of them into someone's baggage at an airport. I left one outside a hospital. I gave one to a couple who couldn't have kids. I tried to split you all up, give you all a better chance of survival. And I kept you." She squeezed January's hand. "I kept you."

January snatched her hand away. "Is that

supposed to make me feel better? How did you pick? Did I smile at you? Was I the one who cried the least? Who made you God? Why did you get to pick?"

"January." I'd heard that warning note in my dad's voice before. "Your mother saved your life and loved you like nobody else. Show some respect."

I watched January's hair turn brilliant, fiery red. I'm pretty sure actual sparks were glowing in it. Her anger was like a coiled serpent, ready to strike, and my dad was the perfect target.

"You can't talk," she snapped. "You're hardly the epitome of perfect parenting, Mr. Marsh. You left your son when he was ten years old and you never got in touch. You've got a lot in common with my 'mother.' Neither of you gives a crap about your kids."

The words seemed to glance off Dad, but I could see the hurt in his eyes as he turned to me. "Is that how you feel?"

"Forget it," I muttered. "I really don't want to talk about this right now."

"Damn right." January shot me a look. "You coming?"

"Where to?" Was she suggesting we just jump from a moving car? And go where? In spite of the niggling feeling that she was right about my dad, I didn't want to just leave him. This was the most time I'd spent with him in years.

"Who cares? We're better off alone. They both dumped us once, so they'll dump us again. Stop the car." She barked the last sentence at my dad and I was torn between respect and the uneasy feeling she was going too far.

"January." My dad's voice was level. He was back in control again. "That's enough. This isn't something anyone will be facing alone. We need to pool our resources. I don't care if you think I'm the devil himself—I'm not letting my son out of my sight until I know he's safe. And that goes for you too. So stay in the car, pull yourself together, and let's deal with this crap."

I watched January's eyes bounce from him to me and back to him again. She hesitated, and I half expected her to shout and scream and tell my dad to go and screw himself. She didn't. She mumbled an apology and let go of the door handle.

Her hair was pink as she looked down at the floor.

Chapter Sixteen

Two to three teaspoons of raw nutmeg can cause hallucinations, convulsions, and paranoia—and, in rare cases, kill people.

"I say we move on. Reinvent ourselves again. Change both our names this time." Jess was looking at January. "Do you like the sound of Storm? I do."

Dad took his eyes off the road for a moment to look at Jess like she was one step away from completely unhinged. "That's no life for a teenage girl," he said, softly.

"At least she's alive," Jess shot back.

January and I were still sitting in the back seat. I wanted to catch her eye, but she was looking steadily out of the window. Her hand was resting on the middle seat and I could have gently brushed her fingers. I could have taken her hand in mine. I could have tried to show her that she wasn't alone in this. But, me being me, I was worried she'd snatch her hand away and that would hurt. So I kept mine to myself. Real brave, huh? Look at Leon Marsh, folks. Can kill two guys, but can't bring himself to be vulnerable with the girl he likes. Just thinking of the dead men made my stomach clench inside me. I could still see their lifeless eyes, goggling up at me. Jess had insisted we stash them in the trunk of the car and take them with us, in case someone else found them and raised the alarm. (Have you ever tried lifting a bulky dead man into the trunk of a car? I wouldn't recommend it as a pleasant way to spend an evening. On the plus side, that was my workout for the day done. Dead men weigh a ton.)

"Look, I know it's none of my business, but don't you think we've all done enough running away from the problem? It's time to meet this head on. Okay, we can't go to the police. What can we do?" My dad looked around at us all, as if one of us had the answer to all those questions and had just decided to keep it a secret for now.

"Against these guys?" Jess said. "Very little! I don't think you appreciate the gravity of this situation. What went on in that laboratory was highly illegal and absolutely under wraps. They'll do anything to stop their secret getting out and they don't care who they have to kill. Running is the only way."

"And they'll always be one step behind you," countered Dad.

"They got April," I said, in a small voice.

Jess turned around to look at us. "April?"

"One of my 'sisters,' Mom, or did you forget about her?" snapped January. "April Tyler. Reported missing from her home shortly after revealing to the entire world that her hair does the same thing as mine. Clear enough?"

"I wanted to find her," I said, numbly. "I thought we could save her."

"Maybe we still can, son." Dad patted my knee. "That's why we need a plan."

"We have a plan," Jess said, firmly. "My daughter and I are going to put as much distance between us and them as we can."

"And you're just going to leave April out there with them? We are the only people in the world who know what's happened to her. The police will never find her on their own!" I didn't realize I was shouting until I saw the looks on everyone's faces. "We have to help her."

"I already saved her once," Jess responded. "It was up to her to keep herself safe from then on."

"Wow, that's cold." I glared at her.

"And, in case you missed it, there's no way in hell

I'm going anywhere with you," January coolly informed her. "I don't trust you and I don't think I even know you anymore."

"There's another way," Dad said, thoughtfully.

We all turned to him. *Please, save us. Tell us there's a magical solution for all this, because we're tired of running and we're tired of near-death experiences.*

"Well?" January snapped. "Don't keep us in suspense."

"Right, say we run. That's our choice for the rest of our lives. And I, for once, don't want to bring up my son like that. Not to mention the fact that I'll be running out on my daughters back at home."

"You ran out on me before." I didn't mean to say that. But I couldn't hold it back. The sentence burst out my mouth, every poisonous word so bitterly, brilliantly clear.

Dad looked at me. He hesitated, and then said: "And that's why I'm not going to make that same mistake again."

"What have they got that I haven't, Dad? Seriously?" *Damn it, Leon, don't cry again.* I turned my face out the window, hoping everyone would think I was disinterested, rather than about to bawl my eyes out. Judging by the way January took my hand, I failed. (Also, look how January was brave enough to initiate hand-holding, but I wasn't. That made me feel even worse. Then again, I suppose, for girls as hot as January, the fear of rejection doesn't ever cross their mind.)

"We'll talk about this later," my dad said, gently. "I will explain it to you, and I will do whatever it takes to earn your forgiveness, but, right now, we need to focus on staying alive. Although my plan is somewhat risky."

"Let's hear it then," repeated January.

"Our second option would be to go to the police

but, if, as your mom says, law enforcement are in the pockets of these guys, then that wouldn't do us much good either. So, how about we go and see these guys? Meet them head on."

"I don't think they'll want to sit down over tea and cakes somehow." January's voice dripped with sarcasm. "That's your fantastic plan? Go and have a friendly chat?"

Dad smiled. "Oh, no. Nothing friendly about this. I'm suggesting your mother and I dress up in the dead men's clothes and go to their HQ in disguise. I'm suggesting we infiltrate their organization, bringing you two along as captives, and I'm suggesting we take them down from the inside."

I'd never believed the phrase "you could hear a pin drop" was particularly accurate. Not until that day, sitting in the car, watching the windows steam up from our breath. Not until my father made that ludicrous, insane, dangerous, someone's-been-watching-too-many-spy-films suggestion. Because all I could hear was the sound of our four heartbeats, thump, thump, thumping away.

Then we all started speaking at once.

"You have *got* to be kidding me."

"You said you wanted to keep the kids safe!"

"Dad … are you serious?"

I was the only one he answered. "Deadly serious. Look at the options logically. Do we really have a choice?"

Chapter Seventeen

The English language has no rhymes for "month," "silver," or "purple."

The dead men had no identification on them. But they did have phones. And thumbs. I tried not to be sick as I watched my dad use their fingerprints to unlock the phones and hack his way in.

"How are you at accents?" Jess asked him, with the hint of a smile. "You'll have to do all the talking, just in case any of them happen to recognize me."

"I'll do my best," promised Dad. "If you tell me which number to call. I'm guessing it'll be the number of your old lab?"

"I guess so." Jess took the phone out of his hands and scrolled down. "That one." Her voice was sure and certain. "For sure."

Dad took a deep breath. "Here goes."

On the third ring, the phone was answered. "About time. We thought you were dead."

"Better than that," Dad said, in what has got to be the worst accent in history. "We've got the kid."

It seemed to fool the person at the other end. Their voice crackled, "Mission accomplished. Get yourselves back to base then."

"Should we bring her with us?"

There was a pause and then the voice broke out laughing. "You're kidding, right? Of course bring her with you. That's why you're over there."

"Whereabouts do you want her?"

"Hooper, stop joking around. Bring the kid back to base at Inverhamilton. And quit hanging around, will you? Clark and Mason have already brought the other girl to the airport."

Dad shot me a look. The other girl. Could she be

April?

"Sure thing, boss," he said. "We'll book the flights."

There was another pause. "Hooper, did you get hit on the head? The jet's at the airport. Meet up with Clark and Mason there and fly home. You've already been briefed on all this. Now do me a favor and get off the line. I've got other calls to make and I don't have time to deal with your BS jokes right now."

The line went dead and Dad turned to us. "Clark and Mason sound like they're gonna be trouble."

"Um, hello! Am I the only one who can see the potential problems with this plan?" demanded January. "For starters, no offence, Mr. Leon's Dad, but you and Mom don't look anything like these creepy dead guys. And don't you think Clark and Mason are gonna notice that? For seconds, we don't even know which jet we're going on. There might be more than one. And thirds…" She pointed at me. "These guys killed another kid that got in their way. What makes you think they'd change tactics when it comes to him? He's not getting shot. Not on my watch."

"We'll cross that bridge when we come to it," Dad said, firmly. "Right now, we've got a plane to catch."

****

I'd never flown in a private jet in my life.

My airport experiences consisted of long queues, punctuated with shrieking babies and jostling adults. Duty-free alcohol and aftershave, glittering from shiny shelves. Neat and tidy air hostesses, the kind of girls you could never imagine getting drunk at parties or going to nightclubs. Cramped seats, sandwiched between strangers, listening to the monotonous soundtrack of snoring, screaming, and sick noises. If you were lucky enough to get a window seat, your ears were probably popping too much to enjoy the view.

And don't even get me started on the food.

So, forgive me for the fact that I was actually enjoying myself.

Yes, our lives were in danger. But… Private. Fricking. Jet.

The first thing I noticed was all the space. The chairs looked like luxury sofas and I could recline them as far back as I wanted without the people behind me complaining (because there was nobody behind me!). Huge windows were on either side of the lounge area, and, when I got bored of pressing my nose against them, I went over to the small kitchen area and poured myself a coffee. There was even a little conference table at a booth, presumably where the evil owner of the jet could conduct evil meetings and make evil plans or whatever he did with his free time. At the very back of the plane was a doorway that, I assumed, led to the bedrooms. I tried the door, but it was locked, so there was no possibility of me taking a nap at forty-thousand feet or however high we were. I'd just have to have a snooze in the luxury leather chairs—what a hardship! Honestly, with all the excess of comfort and snacks and a television I could stream anything I wanted from, I'd almost forgotten to be scared. But January was more cautious. She turned to my dad. "Shouldn't we be treated more … prisonery?" she asked. "In case the other guys get suspicious?"

"There's not many places you can run when you're in the air." He smiled. At least, I think he smiled. It was hard to tell, as most of his features were shrouded in a low-brimmed hat he had picked up at the airport. I'm not sure who he thought it would fool, but at least he was trying. "We'll see what Clark and Mason say when they arrive."

My stomach dropped at the mention of Clark and

Mason. Up until now, I'd been almost enjoying myself. Getting through security had been an absolute blast (there wasn't any. Turns out when you've got a private jet, you're apparently trusted not to bring anything you shouldn't with you. Other than kidnapped kids, of course). Nobody seemed to have recognized that my dad and Jess weren't who they were supposed to be and we never even saw the pilot, tucked away in the cockpit. And, even though I'd been worried we'd pick the wrong jet or something, it had been easy: someone had guided us onto the runway and it was the only one sitting there, like some giant, stranded whale that had washed ashore. The whole plan was going ridiculously smoothly.

Right on cue, the two thugs appeared. "Where's Carter?" they asked, unconsciously referring to Jess, who must have put on Carter's clothes.

"In the bathroom," my dad replied. "He's not feeling too well." We had decided it would be easier if Jess kept well out of the way, so she had been relegated to the lavatory with strict instructions to stay there. She also had my gun with her, the gun I'd used to shoot the real Carter and Hooper.

I was still getting flashbacks that no amount of private aircraft luxury could stop.

But something distracted me. Behind the men trailed a small girl, with a terrified expression in her big eyes. She looked like January. Perhaps not physically, although her hair had that same electric aura about it, but her expression was like January's. There was something about the darkness in both their eyes that suggested they'd seen things no kid ever should—and somehow survived. I remembered the way January had looked us all dead in the eyes on her first day of class. Like she was ready to attack anyone who got in her way. This girl had that same steady, deadly gaze. And she was looking straight at me. My skin trembled, goosebumps dimpling my arms. Electricity was crackling in the air, static standing my hair on end. "April."

I didn't know I'd said her name out loud until her eyes turned from angry to puzzled. "How do you know?"

"Stop talking." Clark, or maybe it was Mason, looked at my dad. "Hooper, who is this one?"

I could have cursed myself for going and opening my big mouth. Why did I have to draw attention to myself? Now the men were looking at me, suspicion written all over their faces. What if they shot me, the way their friends had effortlessly shot Ginger? My body tensed, bracing for a rain of bullets. Dad was scratching his head and shrugging, presumably thinking what to say that wouldn't make Clark and Mason suspicious. But the awkward silence was more suspicious than anything else and I had no idea how to diffuse the situation.

It was April who broke the heavy silence. "He's got abilities too."

I don't know what I expected, but it wasn't that. I opened my mouth to protest but no words came out.

"He can't have. Twelve girls. It was twelve girls…" Mason trailed off as he looked at me. "Wasn't it?" He looked at Clark for backup.

"I guess there could have been a mix-up somewhere. Ours not to reason why and all that." He walked over to me and pushed his face into mine. I could feel his breath tickle my nose and see every red vein in his eyes. "So what are your powers then, kid?"

"He can read minds."

Every eye turned to April. She was standing taller and her voice rang out with confidence. "Telepathy." She jerked her head in an emphatic nod, looking straight at me.

This time, her lips didn't move, and yet I heard

her voice inside my head. *Just play along.* Before I could react, Mason swaggered over to me. Something about the expression on his face made my skin crawl.

"Oh, can you now?" Mason smiled, showing a gold tooth. "Well, tell me, kid, what am I thinking now?"

I closed my eyes and pretended to think. "I need to align myself with the astral vibrations…" I muttered.

Don't overdo it, Leon. Her voice was in my head again. How was she doing it? I could hear her, but not with my ears. She was a headache, she was a migraine, she was tinnitus. *He's thinking: "I wonder if my wife is sleeping with my neighbor while I'm over here."*

I opened my eyes. "What will you do if she is, Mason?"

"Is what?" He took a step back, looking uncertain.

"Sleeping with your neighbor. You think your wife is cheating on you. What will you do if she is?" I kept my gaze fixed on him, staring him down.

Mason's face went white. "Get this kid out of my sight, he's a creep." He barged past me and left the room.

April's eyes never left mine.

Chapter Eighteen

The three main cloud types are stratus, cumulus, and cirrus.

When I was a kid, I was obsessed with clouds. I would lie on my back, stretching my hands to the sky, trying to catch them in my fingers. When the mist hung low, I would walk in it, feeling the dampness on my face, trying to hold it in my hands.

I cried every time it slipped through my fingers.

My mom got bored of me coming home in tears every time it was misty, and my dad got bored of me complaining, so he took me on a hill walk and we stood on the edge of the world surrounded by clouds.

I trapped a cloud in a plastic box and held it in the air like a triumphant athlete. I had my cloud.

I was stupid, and very young, but I expected it would always be a cloud. I thought I could keep it for the rest of my life. I planned show it to Sam and James and Ginger. I'd maybe even lend it to the local museum, if they asked very nicely. I'd be the boy who had his very own cloud. It would always live in my plastic box, puffy and plump and perfectly white.

When we reached the bottom of the hill, all I had in my box was a pool of liquid, as if the cloud had vanished, leaving only its tears behind.

I don't know why I was thinking about my cloud-catching days just then. Maybe it was because I was surrounded by clouds.

Or maybe it was that same old feeling of something slipping right through my fingers.

How had she done that? How had she reached inside my mind and spoken to me?

My dad was sitting in a booth by himself. Clark and Mason were nowhere to be seen. It was now or never.

For all I knew, in an hour's time, we could all be dead.

I left the girls and walked over to my dad, my heart beating faster with every step. "Why did you leave us?" I asked.

He looked up at me, his eyes dark under the brim of his hat. "I…"

"And don't give me any of that crap about adults growing apart and, while they might stop loving each other, they'll never stop loving their kid. Because we both know you stopped loving me."

"I didn't, son."

"Utter crap!" I slammed my fist on the chair beside me. "If you love someone, you stay in touch with them. You remember their birthday! You don't move hundreds of miles away and never speak to them again! And don't tell me it's because you don't like kids or because you don't know what to do with them, because you seem to be doing a perfectly good job with your new family!" I hadn't realized how angry I was until the words poured out of me. I was shaking. I took a deep, ragged breath. "All I'm asking is why you left me, but not them. Seriously? What do they have that I don't?"

"Your mom and I had been having problems for years, okay? She's a difficult woman to live with. You, of all people, should know that. She's moody and angry and nothing I ever did was good enough for her. And Suzanne was just different. Everything I did was more than good enough. She looks at me like I'm her whole world and everything she's ever wanted. Do you have any idea how good that feels? And every time I tried to get in touch with you, your mom turned it into a war. I wanted us all to do stuff as a family. I wanted you to be a brother to my girls. But your mom made that totally impossible, so it was easier just to let you two get on with your lives while I got on with mine."

My shoulders slumped. "So that's the reason then? Because it was easier?"

"Don't take it the wrong way, son. And I'm here now, aren't I? Where's your mom? Do you think she's even noticed you're out of the house?" There was an edge to his voice that just made me even angrier.

"She's not perfect, but she never ran out on me!" I yelled.

"Keep your voice down!"

"You know, you really had me fooled for a second. When you came and found me, I actually thought maybe you cared." My laugh was as bitter as autumn berries.

"Of course I care. Do you think I'd be here, risking my life, if I didn't? I'm not trying to make this a contest between me and your mom. I'm not trying to say I'm better than her. I'm just saying she made things very difficult and I did what I thought was best at the time. I couldn't keep putting Suzanne and the girls through those excruciating meetings."

"What meetings? There was only one!" I shot back. He just raised an eyebrow at me, like I was missing the point. I sighed. He was probably right. My mom had ruined that day for everyone. She was a bit difficult sometimes. But she had always loved me. Did my dad? I wanted to believe so.

"I'm sorry, okay? I'll make it up to you in future. We'll meet up, we'll go out. You can stay with us during the holidays. We will spend more time together."

"Promise?" I asked, as if I was a little kid again.

"I promise. Now go back and sit with the girls, otherwise those guys might get suspicious if they come out and see us talking."

I joined January and April, feeling as if someone had knocked all the air out of my body.

January reached over and took my hand. "It'll be okay," she whispered.

"Will it?" We both turned our heads to stare at the girl across the row. She was smaller than January, with freckles splashed over her face and dimples when she smiled. Her hair was yellow and tied back in a loose ponytail. She lifted her head and stared back at us. *I'm not a freak, you know.* I couldn't help starting in surprise. I glanced at January. Had she heard it too, or was it just me?

April uncrossed her legs and came over to sit opposite us. "I'm not a freak." This time her lips moved. She glanced at January. "You, of all people, should know that."

"I don't want to talk to you." January folded her arms and looked the other way.

"Why not? We're all prisoners here. We might as well get along." April turned to smile at me.

I hesitated. January's hair was turning green. Green for jealous? I still hadn't figured out what all her colors meant and I didn't see why she would be jealous of April.

She hates me, doesn't she? April was smiling at me and I couldn't help but smile back, feeling a stab of guilt when I looked back at January's hunched shoulders and folded arms. I shot April an apologetic look and she shrugged and grinned.

"What's it like, reading minds?" I whispered, in case the men overheard. "Is it really cool? Can you cheat on tests at school and stuff?"

She shot me a pitying look. "You can use it for *way* cooler stuff than that."

"Like what?"

"Like … when you're behind someone at an ATM and you just so happen to hear them thinking what their

PIN is and you just so happen to swipe their card… That kind of cool."

"Great," muttered January to me. "Your new friend's a thief."

April just smiled. "Whatever. You're no angel, January Hill."

"Oh, and what's that supposed to mean?" January whipped round. Her hair was smoldering red.

April's smile died. "See that thing you thought of just there? That's what I was meaning." She leaned forward. "Don't. You won't win." January's hair shot out and seized April's wrist. April just laughed. "Seriously? Did you forget they gave me that ability too?"

"I've had more practice, though." January's grip didn't loosen, and with another thick strand of hair she reached for April's long yellow pony tail.

"January, don't…" For the first time, I saw fear in April's eyes.

The second January's hair connected with April's, there was a loud bang and the two girls were violently forced apart. The smell of burning filled my lungs.

"Oh! That hurt!" January clutched her hair. The ends were frazzled.

April just shook her head. "Seriously? Did you seriously think that would work?"

"What the hell just happened?" boomed my dad.

April switched on her 100-watt smile. "Nothing, sir. A small accident with a lighter."

Dad nodded. "See it doesn't happen again." He went back to his chair.

"You can't fight me, so I suggest we just get along," April said to January with a shrug.

"Fine," spat January. "But let it be known I don't trust you and I don't like you."

"And let it be known I really don't care."

"April, you seem like a smart girl," I said. "So why did you make the biggest mistake of your life last week?"

She blinked at me. "Huh?"

"Why did you tell the whole world your hair does that … thing?"

"I wanted people to know." She shrugged. "I figured if people knew, I might get film offers. Modelling contracts. I might get famous, you know? Mary and Jamie wanted me to keep it a secret. Said if anyone found out, they might want to exploit me. Well, yeah, sorry, that's not the life I want. Once I get famous, I'll have bodyguards, anyway." She broke off as she realized we were both staring at her in disbelief. "What?"

"April, you must know there's something a lot bigger going on than just a couple of girls with color-changing hair here…" I said.

"Yeah, top secret plot, blah, blah, genetic enhancement, blah, blah, blah. I listened to January's mom's thoughts as soon as she slunk on the plane. Good thing she's hiding in the bathroom because the guilt was just radiating off her and everyone would be sure to spot it. I don't care about all of that spy crap. Conspiracy theories and whatever. We'll have a fight, we'll win—the good guys always do—and then our lives will go back to normal and I can focus on getting rich and famous. 'Kay?" She plopped her feet onto the seat opposite her and crossed her legs.

"Shallow much?" muttered January.

"Nope. Focused. Determined. I know what I want. Don't you wish you did too?"

I couldn't help smiling. There was something so huge about April's personality. Huge and complex. I wondered if anyone ever got to know the real April. Or was everyone just a means to an end? But she had saved my ass the moment she got on the plane and I owed her for that.

"Leon?" She touched my arm. "There's something you need to know."

"What?"

"It's about your dad."

I didn't get to hear what she was going to say because at that moment there was a terrifying jolt and, out of the window, I could see lights sweeping past us.

Dad appeared, flashing a wolfish grin at us. "Kids? We've arrived."

ROZ MACLAREN

Chapter Nineteen

Koalas have such similar fingerprints to humans that they could easily be confused at a crime scene.

April was tugging on my arm. *Leon, it's really important...*

"Shh!" I cut her off. Clark and Mason were emerging from their rooms.

But, Leon...

"Right, you lot, off we go," Mason said. He pointed threateningly at a bulge in his coat pocket. "Remember we're all armed, so don't get any bright ideas about escaping."

A blast of icy cold air nearly knocked me off my feet as I walked down the steps. In the dark, I felt for January's hand. I don't know what I had expected to happen. Maybe I thought my father would magically manage to overpower Clark and Mason and then take over the plane and fly somewhere safe. (Never mind the fact that, to the best of my knowledge, he had never flown a plane before.)

You've been watching too many spy thrillers.

Get out of my head, April. I framed the thought in my head, hoping she could hear me. I could almost hear her laughing in response.

How well do you know your dad?

I stumbled. *What?*

January tightened her grip on my hand. "It's okay."

I'm just asking. I detect a lot of conflicted emotions in your mind when you think of him.

Do me a favor and stop detecting.

April was an earworm, a virus. Boring into my brain, exploring every secret thought. I could picture her working her away among my neurons and impulses. Picking up my thoughts and turning them over in her hands, like they were pebbles on the beach for her to collect. Like she had every right to explore.

It's kind of funny, Leon, but you're the only one who has ever been aware of me. You can feel me listening to your thoughts, can't you? Nobody else ever could.

I concentrated my thoughts. *What about my dad? What were you trying to say about him?*

I'm trying to say that I've been able to read pretty much everyone's mind, except his and I don't know why. Every time I go to read his mind, he thinks of random stuff, like plants or the ocean or something completely irrelevant. I don't know if someone's warned him I can read minds and he's deliberately stopping me or if he just has a bizarre appreciation for botany, but I'm trying to say he's blocked me—whether he means to or not. And I find that very suspicious.

My shoulders instantly relaxed. So what if my dad was thinking of plants? That didn't make him dangerous. I'd reached the end of the stairs. I turned back to April. "Coincidence."

"Are you sure?" She lifted an eyebrow. "I'm just asking." *How well do you really know him?*

"Stop it, stop it!" I clamped my hands over my ears.

That won't do any good. I'm in your head, remember? Her voice was as loud as ever. *Look, I'm not saying anything bad about him. And I can see you two have been estranged for a good few years now.*

"What's wrong?" January was peering at me, concerned. She whipped round to face April. "What are you doing to him?"

April rolled her eyes. "Relax."

"Enough talk. Into the van." Clark jerked his

thumb at a battered pickup.

The three of us tumbled into the back of a large van. There were no windows, which gave me instant claustrophobia. The cabin was separated from the back by a sheet of thick glass, blocking out the sounds from the front and making me feel weirdly disconnected from the outside world. I watched January's mom and my dad get in the front, along with Clark and Mason. Jess had her hat pulled low over her face and kept her eyes on the ground. All the same, a prickle of fear slithered up my spine. Would she and my dad manage to keep up their disguise? Or would we all be killed?

All I knew was that January's hand was still in mine and I never wanted to let it go.

April had noticed this. "Are you two going out?" she wanted to know.

I wanted to see what January would say, so I didn't reply. Perhaps she wanted to see what I would say, because she didn't speak either and there was an awkward silence. I could almost hear April rolling her eyes. She mimed a loud and increasingly graphic vomiting display.

"See this whole reading minds thing…" January said. "Can you just go into a person's head and see everything they've ever thought? All their memories and stuff? Or can you only see what they're thinking at that particular moment?"

April smirked. "Bit of both. Depends how susceptible the person is. With some people, I can only listen to their active thoughts. With others, I can get access to pretty much everything. Active thoughts are the easiest by far. Strong emotions, that kind of thing."

"How reassuring," January said, sarcastically.

"She does love you, you know. Your mom. I know you're angry with her for not telling you the full story.

She did what she had to do." April gave January a superior smile.

"Seriously, don't go there." January's tone was dark and angry. I could see her hair glowing faintly in the dark. Red.

"Guys, we need to talk about our plan," I said. "And seeing as two of you have superpowers, you need to work together—for all our sakes. Even if you hate each other's guts, okay?"

"Yes, leader," April replied, with a hint of sarcasm. "What do you suggest we do?"

"My dad's plan is to somehow infiltrate the laboratory and then, I'm guessing, take control somehow? Destroy it? I don't even know. We have to do that, otherwise they'll just keep coming after us all. And you two will be in danger for the rest of your lives."

"I think we can take care of ourselves," April shrugged. "Remind me again what your superpower is?"

"My superpower is keeping you two safe," I said, firmly. "Whatever it takes."

Even in the dark, I could see January's hair was changing color, turning to soft gold. Her hand tightened in mine. I knew that, whatever the future would bring, I would have an ally in January.

****

The doors were wrenched open and blinding light flooded into the van. We all blinked and squinted.

"Out, kids," ordered my dad. I couldn't meet his eyes properly. After our shouting match on the plane and after what April had said… But maybe she was lying. Maybe she was messing with my head, trying to make me doubt myself, trying to play with me.

How well do you really know your dad? she had asked.

How well can you really know someone after a

four-year absence? How well do you really know anyone, even when you live with them?

The air may have been colder out here. But that wasn't the only reason why a shiver went through my soul. Standing in front of us was a large, oblong-shaped building that looked distinctly like a prison. It must have had about six stories, all with rows of gaping windows. I glanced behind me, my eyes following the road we had driven along to get here. It snaked and curved for what seemed like miles. There was nothing behind us—no buildings, no sign of life, not so much as a road sign. Only desolate plains, brown and dusty, with the occasional defeated-looking tree. I half-expected the obligatory tangle of tumbleweed to go bouncing by. It was the perfect place to bring people if you didn't want them to be found.

"That must be the laboratory," whispered April.

It loomed above us like the villain in a sci-fi film. The faint buzz of electricity filling the air, crawling through the power lines over our heads. Two armed guards stood outside a set of doors. I could feel their eyes on me as we walked over. Clark flashed some ID at them and they stood aside to let us past.

I wondered, with my usual overdramatic tendency, if this would be the last building I'd ever walk into before I died.

ROZ MACLAREN

Chapter Twenty

Polar bears are left-handed. (Or should that be left-pawed?)

So was the man behind the desk. The big cheese, presumably. The guy we had to take down, if we wanted survive. The villain of the piece. You get the idea.

Unfortunately, he didn't look overly villainous. In fact, he looked vaguely familiar. Or maybe it was just that he looked quite ordinary. There was no eyepatch. No hook for a hand. He looked like an everyday guy. Someone's uncle. Someone's dad.

How stupid I was. How quickly I forgot the obvious. *Just because you're someone's dad doesn't stop you being the villain.*

I recognized him. I was growing certain of that, even though it didn't make any sense. How could I recognize him? I'd never been here before. I'd never seen him before. I didn't think he'd been on television or in the news. But I had seen his face, and fairly recently. I could feel the niggle of a half memory dancing around in my brain, always just slipping through my fingers.

"Well, Mike, you made it," the villain was saying.

It took me a second to process the words. It took me even longer to understand the meaning.

How did he know my dad's real name?

Well done, you've finally asked the right question. April's voice filled my head.

My dad was smiling at the big cheese. "Yes, sir, we made it. Two girls safely delivered." He was using his Serious Voice, the kind he used on the phone with clients when he wanted them to think he had everything under control. I blinked up at him, still wondering why he was being so friendly to the enemy, still so slow on the uptake.

Jess was staring at him too, as if she couldn't quite believe her ears. "What's going on, Mike?" she asked, uncertainly, apparently forgetting she wasn't supposed to speak. Her eyes were locked on my dad.

"Oh, this is actually Hair Girl's mother," Dad said, gesturing at her.

"We know each other. Hello, Jennifer." The man behind the desk smirked and folded his arms. "I thought you'd gone to earth like some frightened animal. Bet you never thought you'd end up back here again."

"Jennifer?" echoed January. "Who's Jennifer?"

"Me," Jess said, wearily, pulling the hat off her head and letting her blonde hair fall free. "Hello, Ted," she said, glaring at the man behind the desk. "Long time no see."

A lightning bolt of realization flashed through my brain. I remembered where I knew the man from. Those dark, snake-cold eyes, the wisps of grey hair above a puffy face. "That's the man in your drawing!"

January swallowed. "Is he my dad?"

Jess' eyes widened. "Oh, sweetie, no. Is that what you thought?"

January nodded. "I found his photograph in your files. I thought maybe he'd given me up for adoption or something."

"I had his photograph because we used to work together." Jess folded her arms and glared at Ted. "Until I realized exactly what he was up to and what levels he'd sink to in order to achieve his 'vision.'"

"What vision?" April asked.

Ted smirked. "The vision of making this world a better place. Of pushing the realms of possibility and creating new life, exactly the way I want it."

"Blah, blah, blah," Jess said, rudely. "You're not

the first megalomaniac who thinks they can play God and, unfortunately, you won't be the last. I should have stopped you all those years ago when I had the chance, instead of running."

"You ran to keep January safe," I reminded her. "You ran because you had a baby girl to look after."

Ted leaned forwards, resting his chin on his palm. "You did pretty well to elude me all these years."

"What can I say? Maybe you should have looked harder." Jess glared at my dad. "Mike, what's going on? Whatever Ted's promised you, I guarantee he won't deliver. He'll say whatever he needs to in order to get what he wants."

My dad shrugged and looked away. "I'm just doing what I have to do to protect my family."

"You liar." The power of speech had deserted me, but not, apparently, January. She wrenched herself free of Clark and marched up to my dad. "You traitor!"

My dad sighed. "I don't have to justify anything to you, but I'm not a traitor. I'm doing what I have to do to keep my kids safe. Including Leon. You're just a freak, manufactured in a lab. It's only right to put you back where you came from."

"Don't you dare talk to her like that." It was my turn to break free and stand in front of my dad. "I'd far rather have January in my life than you. All that crap you told me on the plane—that was just to keep me from making a fuss. You didn't mean any of it, did you? You don't give a hoot about me—you never did!"

My dad rolled his eyes. Actual eye rolling. Like I didn't even matter enough to get angry with. I was that unimportant to him. "Oh, the melodrama. We'll discuss this at home, okay? Not now."

Ted pulled out a gun from his desk drawer, whistling slowly. His movements were so casual, it was almost relaxing to watch him flick the revolver cylinder open and slide bullets in every chamber. He was whistling an old pop tune from the 1950s.

He was still whistling when he lifted the revolver and fired straight at Jess.

It was all done so quickly, so naturally. As if Ted didn't have to think about it. Jess looked down at her front. Blood was seeping through a wound in her chest. Her eyes were wide.

My body froze. The echo of the gunshot was still ringing in my ears. January was moving, running over to her mother. Jess' legs crumpled and January caught her as she fell.

"You won't save her," Ted said. "I got her straight through the heart. I never miss. Should have done that fourteen years ago when I had the chance. Would have saved all this aggro."

Tears shone in January's eyes as she clutched her mother, cradling her head in her arms. "Please don't leave me, please don't die," she whispered.

Jess managed a watery grin. "It's all right," she slurred. She winced with every word. "I … I'm so proud of you."

It wasn't like in the movies where the dying character slumps dramatically to the side and everyone knows they've died and there's a moment of silence to reflect on the character's noble sacrifice. In real life, Jess just went rigid. Her eyes stared unseeingly up at the ceiling. And we weren't allowed any time to process what had just happened, that the man who looked like someone's friendly old uncle had just casually killed Jess as easily as he might squash a bug. With about as much regret. Because Clark was hauling January to her feet, even though she was fighting him all the way. "Shall I get this lot out of here, sir?" he asked Ted.

"No way." January planted her feet on the ground. "If you want me dead, you're going to have to kill me here."

Ted roared with laughter. "Want you dead? What makes you think I want you dead? You're far too valuable to kill." He reached over to slowly touch the tips of January's hair. "I've spent years tracking you down. Trying to find you again. The woman you think of as your mother stole you away from me. But I have you back. I certainly don't want you dead."

"What about Ginger?" I croaked.

Ted looked quizzically at me. "Ginger…?"

"Ginger Monroe. Our friend. Your guys killed her." January's words came out as a snarl.

"Oh, the girl we thought was you at first? Ah yes, I must admit, my boys were a bit trigger-happy. Their instructions were to take you somewhere safe for questioning, just to double check you absolutely were the right girl. But they took her, of course. I'm led to understand she had vibrant hair and my idiotic minions just assumed she was you. And, when they found she wasn't you…" Ted mimed a throat-slashing motion. "Collateral damage, I'm afraid."

"You're sick," I spat.

The avuncular villain nodded. "All great scientific visionaries are misunderstood in their own time." To his men, he said, "Take them away and find a cell for each of them."

They roughly grabbed all three of us by the shoulders and tried to lead us out of the room.

My dad held up his hand. "Wait. Leon's not part of the deal."

"But he's got the powers," Mason chimed in. "He read my mind."

Dad shook his head. "He's my son. I assure you

he's got no powers. I only brought him along so the girls would come quietly."

January's hand found mine. And April, who had also broken out of the men's grasp, took my other hand. We stood, defiantly, a tiny human chain, facing our enemies. I hoped my dad couldn't see the hurt in my eyes. I didn't want him to know he had taken my heart out of my chest and crushed it into a million pieces.

"Take the girls away," ordered the man behind the desk. "Leave the boy."

Clark and Mason dragged the girls, kicking and biting, out of the door. January and April were using their hair to fight back, until Clark pressed his gun into April's temple and screamed "If you don't stop it, I'll kill you right now!" Something about the look in his eyes left me in no doubt that he meant what he said. April turned and looked straight at me. *End this.*

I didn't have time to ask her what she meant. She was gone. They were both gone.

"You've done very well," Ted said. "There are still more girls to find, if you're interested in the job, but we can talk about that later. Take your boy home and I'll be in touch with more details."

"Yes, Ted." My dad clapped a hand on my shoulder. "Let's go, kid."

I couldn't move. "Please, Ted."

The man behind the desk looked at me. "What is it, lad?"

I asked a question I wasn't sure I wanted the answer to. "What will you do with them? January and April?"

"I'd tell you, but I'd have to kill you." Ted laughed.

My fists clenched. I hated it when people joked during important moments. "No, seriously. They're my friends. I need to know."

Ted sighed. "They're not anyone's friends. They're manufactured weapons that we have recovered."

"They were born," I persisted. "They were born in a hospital in Inverhamilton. You took them from their parents. They're human."

"Someone's done his homework." Ted grinned.

"Is everything a great big joke to you?" I demanded. "You think you can just rip someone's kids away from them, turn them into weapons, and then kill to get them back and you think that's okay?"

Ted looked over my head at my dad. "I think it's past your son's bedtime."

And, just like that, we were dismissed.

April's words were still echoing in my mind. I wasn't sure if she was repeating them to me or if they'd just had a deep impact.

End this.

It was on me now. I was the only one still free. I was the only one who could do it.

End this.

ROZ MACLAREN

Chapter Twenty-One

You can lead a cow up stairs—but not back down stairs!

"How could you?" We were barely out of the office before the words burst out of my lips. "How could you betray us all like that?"

My dad caught hold of my shoulders and knelt down beside me, like I was a kid of five. "I did what I had to do to protect my family. Suzanne rang me in hysterics, saying you'd come and were acting weirdly. I came back home, then you left. Five minutes afterwards two hit men in suits come bounding up to the door looking for you. I knew you'd got into some kind of mess, but I didn't know what, so I made a deal: I'd help the men get that girl, if they'd leave you, Suzanne, and the kids alone. Turns out, I got lucky—two girls for the price of one. And I made a deal with Ted, not just to keep my family safe, but he's going to pay me a ton of money. I'll be able to send my girls to good schools. I'll be able to take you out to lunch somewhere decent."

"Don't kid yourself," I sneered. "You didn't do any of this for me. You did it all for yourself. You think I care where we go for lunch or if we just have a sandwich on a park bench? I'd have given everything I had for you to come and see me and spend some quality time with me, just once, just once! But you never did."

"We've been over this," my dad said, wearily. "Let's go." He paced down the long corridor. "We need to get out of here before they change their minds."

"Screw you, Mike." It was the first time I'd called him by his own name. "January and April are more family to me than you ever were—and you've just made the biggest mistake of your life. Even if I do get out of this alive, I don't want anything more to do with you. Mom was right all along."

Dad glared at me. "Stop it! You don't realize who you're dealing with here."

I looked him up and down. "I think I do."

"I don't mean me! One false move and you and I could be on the wrong end of a gun. I gave them my word you were on our side—the right side."

I sighed, kicking at the ground with the toe of my shoe. Suddenly, I hugged my dad, breathing in the nearly forgotten scent of his aftershave. I closed my eyes. "I'm sorry, Dad."

"What for?"

I still held him. I thought back over all the years of hugs I'd never had. My arms slipped lower until I pulled back. "I'm sorry for believing you ever gave a crap about me and my feelings." I had what I came for. The gun from his pocket was now in my hand. "You're right, Dad. You are on the wrong end of a gun."

"Leon…" He held up his hands. "Don't be stupid… You'd never shoot me."

"Nope." Without warning, I wrenched a nearby door that was slightly ajar, slamming it as hard as I could into my father's head. "But I would knock you out and give myself a chance to find my friends and escape," I said, to his unconscious form as he slumped to the ground.

A voice called out from behind me. "Any chance you could take me with you?"

I jumped as I realized I'd opened the door to a room that wasn't empty. A girl was watching me with inquisitive eyes. She was handcuffed to a chair, but somehow made it look like the height of fashion. She had long purple hair and large dark eyes. She looked about sixteen.

I raised my eyebrows. "Let me guess," I said. "You have magic hair too?"

She rolled her eyes. "For goodness' sake, why does everyone keep asking me that? No, you idiot. Not magic hair. I mean, I think they tried to give me magic hair and failed because, last time I checked, purple wasn't a naturally occurring pigment. But, no, I've got a different gift and it's far more spectacular than chameleon hair. Undo me and I might show it to you. The keys are over there. And hurry! The scientists left the door open—that means they'll be back at any moment."

I cautiously stepped into the room and found the keys. She slipped out of her handcuffs and rubbed her wrists before extending a hand.

I shook it. "Leon Marsh."

"June. Just June. And I haven't the faintest idea what's going on, so fill me in."

I smiled. "It's a long story."

"My favorite kind."

****

"So, let me get this straight. You've just knocked your father out and we're going to leave him there and now we're looking for two other girls, who happen to have similar powers to mine, and then we're making a break for freedom?" June's brow wrinkled. "Did I miss anything?"

She was struggling to keep up as I power walked down the long corridors. "Yep, you've got it, and we don't have much time as they'll notice my dad hasn't left yet. Do you have any idea where they might keep their prisoners in this place?"

June shook her head. "Nope. They brought me in yesterday, strapped me to that chair, and asked me all kinds of questions. Tested me a lot."

"Did you resist?"

She snorted. "Screw that, man. I got the impression if I didn't do exactly as I was told, I'd get my head blown off. I cooperated my ass off."

I couldn't help laughing. It amazed me how these three girls were more or less sisters, given the way they had been enhanced in the lab, but so incredibly different. January—a perfect mix of strength and vulnerability. April, who had absolutely no filter and a razor-sharp wit, who saved my ass when she didn't have to. And now June—tough, beautiful June with a mysterious power.

"I don't suppose you can read minds, can you?" I asked, hopefully. "Then you can read the girls' and find out where they're being kept?"

"Nope," June replied, as we wandered down yet another featureless corridor. "Sorry."

"So, what can you do?"

June just smiled. "I'll show you when the time is right."

Leon...

Her voice was so vivid, I turned round to look for her. *April?*

We're on Sub-level Three, underground. They put us in separate rooms, but I just broke us out.

I concentrated my mind, framing the words in my head. *You broke out? How?*

I'll tell you when I see you. Sufficient to say, I was awesome.

I grinned. *Humble as ever. Are you all right?*

As all right as you can be when you've just been abducted by mad scientists.

I couldn't help laughing.

"What's so funny?" asked June.

Who's that?

"Your sister," I said, in answer to both. "Your sister."

Chapter Twenty-Two

Stonehenge is older than the pyramids.

"Took you long enough." Typical April. We'd infiltrated a secret laboratory, avoided guards and blundered our way down to Sub-level Three, and, still, she was unfazed. If a meteor struck Earth, she'd only raise an eyebrow.

She and January were standing outside the elevator in Sub-level Three. January unexpectedly wrapped her arms round me and buried her face into my neck. I could feel the whisper of her breath against my skin.

"How did you get out of a locked room?" I demanded.

April smirked and pointed at the fingerprint scanners next to every door. "The scientists who built those thought they were dead clever. They don't just read fingerprints. They read neurological brain waves."

"I don't follow…" Sometimes it's tough being the only ordinary one in the room. The other girls were all nodding like April was making perfect sense. She definitely wasn't to me.

April pointed at her head and winked at me. "I'm a telepath. I basically told the machine I was Ted and it had no reason to suspect otherwise."

"Yeah, now you come to mention it, I do struggle to tell you both apart," I teased.

"We need to move," January cut in. "They could be after us any minute."

"I don't envy their chances." June cocked a hip like she was some kind of secret agent.

January and April looked at each other and then at June. "Jeez, how many more of us are there?" groaned April.

A small sound, a tiny click, came from behind us and we whipped round. Ted and another man were standing there—one of them holding a gun. "Found you," he said, with a toothless smile.

Instinctively, I stepped in front of the girls. I have no idea why—out of all of us, I was definitely the weakest link. But I knew, with total certainty, that I couldn't let anything happen to January.

My heart felt like it was sinking down to my knees. This was how it ended. After all the running, all the fighting, it would end with gunshots and bloodstains.

"You, boy," Ted said. "You faked having powers, didn't you?"

I nodded. "Yes."

"Good to know." He turned to the man with the gun. "Shoot him. We can tell Mike he ran off and escaped. Once that's done, secure the girls." He strolled casually away.

"Ted?" I screamed after him.

"What, boy?" He didn't stop walking. He didn't glance over his shoulder.

"I hope you rot in hell, Ted!" My lungs burned, I screamed so loud.

He half turned and smiled. "Keep me a seat by the fire, kid."

You're expecting one of those scenes like in the movies, where I look at the man with the gun and he looks at me and we stare at each other, retina to retina, pupil to pupil, and then he realizes he can't go through with it and he has an emotional breakdown and we comfort him and gain an ally.

Sorry to disappoint. Because the next thing I was aware of was a gunshot.

I braced, waiting for the pain.

It never came.

She was faster than the bullet. Did she make the conscious choice to save me, or did instinct take over? Did she know she might die in my place?

It was April who was bleeding. It was April who had stepped in front of me.

Surprise flashed across the man's face as he realized his bullet had missed his mark. January stepped in front of me. "You take him down, you take me down."

"Relax, sister." June took several leggy steps forward until she was standing in front of the man. She cupped his chin in one of her hands and then turned to me. "You want to see what I can do?" She turned back to him and locked eyes, pressing her fingertips to his temples. He started screaming and writhing, in obvious terror. June held him in place, smiling a witch-like grin, until she released him and he bolted down the corridor.

"What the hell...?" demanded January, staring in awe at June, who just smirked.

"Um, excuse me, I'm lying here shot..." a small voice reminded us.

"April!" I crouched down beside her.

"It's actually only a flesh wound—I just wanted some attention." She showed me her arm. "Think the bullet's still in there though." Her face had gone very pale.

"We need to get the hell out of here," January said.

"Can you walk?" I asked April.

"It's my arm, not my leg." She was struggling to keep her characteristic sass up—and that alone made me more scared. I helped her to her feet and we hurried along the maze of corridors again, with no real idea of where we were going or who might be around the next bend.

"Why did you do it?" I asked her.

"Um, duh. He was going to kill you."

"April, I'm serious. Why did you do it?"

She gave me a sad little look, the kind of look a cat gives a bird it will never catch. "Why do you think I did it?"

"Um, guys?" June turned around. "Not to brag, but I've got a plan."

Don't ask me why, but my shoulders instantly relaxed when I heard those words. Yes, I'd known June the grand total of about an hour. Yes, she was completely unhinged. Yes, she had done something mysterious and unspeakable to that man. But did I trust her with my life? Yes. I absolutely did.

I might have been alone with the trust thing. "June, what did you do to that guy?" January asked suspiciously.

June rolled her eyes. "You've got hair, right? She's got hair and telepathy. I've just got telekardia."

"Tele-what now?"

June huffed impatiently. "Can we discuss this later? It's really not that important."

"Nah, I really think it is actually. Whatever you did to that guy, it terrified him." January was inch taller than June and she made the most of it, trying to tower over the other girl, who didn't seem the least bit fazed.

"Tele. Ancient Greek, meaning 'from a distance.' Kardia. Ancient Greek, meaning 'heart.' Do you follow?"

"Not really…"

"Telepathy is transferring conscious thought to another. I can do something similar, but not quite as advanced, I guess. Maybe I was a prototype for April's abilities. Either way, I can make people *feel* things. I can't communicate with them mentally. But I can make them scared, I can make them feel happiness, I can make them feel anger. I can make them feel anything I damn well want. You can't imagine how useful that is when you're in trouble with the teacher and you make them feel happy for no reason at all. You get off quite lightly then." She locked eyes with January. "Or when you're imprisoned in a secret laboratory and you want to scare the guards into letting you go. The possibilities are endless."

"I've never heard of telekardia..." muttered January.

June shrugged. "Maybe they invented it. I don't know, and, right now, I don't care. I told you. I've got a plan."

"And I've got a very bad feeling about this," retorted January.

"And I've got a bullet hole in my frigging arm!" We all turned to look at April, who shrugged. "I'm just saying. I win. Now, let's get the hell out of here."

That was when about twenty men appeared. All of them were holding guns. All of them were pointing at us.

I looked around at the girls and did the only thing I could do. I raised my hands.

ROZ MACLAREN

Chapter Twenty-Three

There's a rare genetic mutation that causes double eyelashes. Elizabeth Taylor was said to have had it.

That was about all I knew about genes—and I wasn't even sure I'd remembered that correctly. Wandering down these endless corridors where all manner of genetic experiments had been carried out made my skin crawl.

"June?" I hissed. "Do something! Use your telekardia."

"I can't use it on everyone." June rolled her eyes. "I have to be touching the person."

I glanced at January. She looked exhausted. Her face was pale and the dark rings under her eyes told me just how much she'd been through in the last few days. Even with her two sisters, there was no way she'd be able to fight off all these men. My heart sank. This really was it.

The walking ended soon. The men separated us from each other and put us into individual cells. I was the last one. A man clamped his hand on my shoulder so hard he almost dislocated it and thrust me into the cold grey cell. I heard the metallic clank of metal as the door slammed shut. I didn't waste my breath calling after the men as they walked away. People always do that in films, don't they? I've never known why. Do they expect the perps to go "Oh sorry, you're right, I'll let you out because you've screamed the place down"? I waited until the sounds of their footsteps echoed away and then I sank to the floor, with my back against the wall.

I could see January in the cell opposite me. She was trying to use her hair to force the cell bars apart. I could see her face turning scarlet with the effort. I wanted to tell her to give up. That we were quite clearly stuck here forever. That, probably tomorrow, those men would come back and they'd kill us.

Is it just me or is anyone else wondering how many times people had to try and escape from this place before they decided to add cells? April's voice in my head was oddly soothing.

January is trying to force her way out using her hair. I focused on transmitting the thought. I could almost hear April chuckle inside my head.

She won't. These bars are nothing if not solid.

If they're going to kill me, why aren't they doing it already?

Can you hear a mental shrug? I wasn't sure but it certainly felt like that's what April was doing. *Who knows? Maybe they're going to wait until morning. Maybe they want you for something. Either way, I suggest you get some sleep. We're going to be in here for a while.*

And if we're not?

Then we've no need to worry because we'll be dead.

****

It was impossible to tell the time when I woke up. Somehow, I'd managed to fall asleep. My back was pressed against the icy stone wall and my lower half was frozen against the equally icy floor. My eyes blinked as I tried to adjust to the darkness.

Footsteps were sounding. Soft, urgent footsteps and the whispery sound of someone feeling their way along the corridor. I could hear the rustle of their clothes pressing against the walls.

"Leon?" a voice whispered. "Are you here?"

"Dad?" I couldn't stop myself answering him. Even though I hated him. Even though the last time I saw him, I'd knocked him out and left him. "What are you doing here?"

A dark shape appeared in front of my cell. Silver glinted in the dim light and I heard the muffled jingle of keys as my dad fumbled with them. "Dad, what are you doing?"

"What's it look like I'm doing?" he muttered. I heard a click as the key turned in the lock. My door swung open with a high-pitched creak. "I stole these keys from Ted's office and I'm getting you out of here."

I folded my arms. I have no idea why, since he wouldn't have been able to see my defensive body language in the darkness. "I'm not going. Not without the girls."

"Leon, don't be a fool!" hissed my dad urgently.

"You can run out on people if you want, Dad. But I'm not going to do that." I lifted my eyes to his. "I know how much it hurts to be the one left behind."

"Is this about me leaving your mother again?" demanded Dad.

I swallowed. "You didn't just leave her. You left *me*."

My dad sighed softly and then walked into the cell. I could feel the warmth of his body as he sat down beside me. The darkness enveloping us felt almost comforting. If I didn't think too hard about the current situation (and the freezing cold stone pressing against my back), I could pretend I was small again and my dad was about to read me a bedtime story before I went to sleep. (Yeah, I know. Silly, right? Still, it's what I was thinking when he sat down beside me.)

"You seem to think your mother was perfect until after I left, don't you?" There was no trace of anger or bitterness in his voice—just a resigned sadness. I picked at the bits of skin around my fingernails, not caring if it hurt or I made it bleed. "Do you have any idea how much

I sheltered you? When your mom didn't make it to work because she had been drinking the night before, I was the one who called in sick for her. I was the one who made dinner for us all. I was the one who saw you got put to bed and had a story told to you."

Anger coursed through my body again. I could feel it, curling through my veins, clenching my hands into fists. "If she was that bad, why did you leave me with her?"

"Because it would have broken her heart if I hadn't!" My dad's voice was raised now, echoing through the corridors. He took a deep breath and then whispered: "I was scared that if I took you, she might do something stupid. But if I left you, then maybe she would get her act together. Maybe you'd give her something to live for, okay? I'm sorry, it just … it felt like the right thing to do at the time. And I know that's nowhere near good enough. I know it sounds like a pathetic excuse for a bad decision. But I was at my wits' end. I had no idea what to do. So, yeah, maybe I did the wrong thing and I'm sorry for that. Really sorry. But if you hang onto this grudge, this chip you carry on your shoulder, then you and I will never be able to put the past behind us. We'll never be able to move on together. I want my son back." He extended his hand. I could see the whiteness of his skin in the dark.

"I still hate you sometimes," I confessed. But I took his hand. And I shook it.

"Hate me all you want. Are you ready to get the hell out of here?" Dad handed me the keys. "You and your friends?"

My face felt like it was going to crack because I was smiling so hard.

****

I stopped smiling when I realized we still had to make our way around the mazelike corridors and get out without being spotted.

"Can you find the way out?" January pleaded with April. "Read someone's mind and tell us what way to go?"

"I'm a telepath, not a satnav," snapped April. But she closed her eyes and a frown creased her forehead. "Sub-Level Four. There's a way out that doesn't involve having to walk past the guards on the front."

"How many frigging sub-levels does this place have?" I wondered.

"Too many," Dad replied. "I got hopelessly lost trying to find you all."

I've always hated elevators. Something about the enclosed space and the shiny four walls that seem to get smaller all the time makes my breath catch in my throat.

January was poking at the buttons, as if that would make the elevator go down faster. June was leaning against the wall, checking her reflection in the mirror. April's eyes found mine. "Are you okay?" she whispered.

Yeah. The girl who had just taken a bullet for me was asking *me* if I was okay. "I'm fine," I whispered back. "Just scared, I guess. How's the wound?"

"Getting sore," she admitted.

"Hey…" June stepped in front of her. "You know, I could help with the pain, if you wanted."

The girls looked at each other. There was an unspoken tension in the air, with all three of them. They were all used to being the most interesting person in the room. Now they'd gone from being unusual to being the norm, one of twelve. And none of them knew how to handle it.

"You can have a go if you want," April said, as the elevator lurched downwards.

June cupped April's face in her hands and leaned

their foreheads together. January looked at me in the mirror. There was something in her gaze I couldn't understand. Something sad, something strong. Something like goodbye.

I was behind the girls, pressed against the wall while June held April. January turned. The mirror image wasn't enough for her. She looked me straight in the eyes. The elevator stopped. The doors twitched. January was out before they were even halfway open. I could see her face, framed between the silver doors. Her eyes never left mine, but I could hear her slamming her fist against the button and the elevator doors were suddenly closing.

I realized too late what she was doing. "January!" I pushed past the girls. "January, what the hell?" The doors were closing as I reached for them. If I could just get one finger in between them, they would reopen. I could stop her. I was inches away, until a wave of golden hair exploded through the gap, pushing my hand away. The elevator doors closed on it and we were lurching back downwards. January's hair was ripping and tearing. I could hear her cry out in pain.

"January!"

April and June were staring at me as I lay on the elevator floor, clutching the remnants of January's beautiful hair.

"Why did she do that?" demanded Dad.

"She didn't want anyone else to risk their lives," April said, softly.

I was fighting with the elevator buttons, punching them over and over again. We were heading resolutely down to the basement, and there was nothing I could do about it. Even if I jumped out the minute the elevator landed, January would be long gone.

"April, can you speak to her?" I demanded. "Can you ask her what the hell she's doing?"

April closed her eyes. "She says she's going to kill Ted and meet us outside. No biggie, she says."

Kill Ted. Of course. I replayed the look in her eyes, that dark, lost look. The kind of look people get when they've nothing left to lose. When they've already lost everything that mattered to them. I knew that look. I'd seen it in the mirror after Dad left. It's the kind of look that means people are dangerous. Reckless. Because they no longer care what happens to them.

But *I* cared. I cared what happened to January. I cared more than anything.

I was stroking her hair in my hands, turning it over and over. It was no longer blonde, but grey. The ends were shriveling up, like leaves in autumn. Curling in on itself, doing the fetal position. Dying. "She doesn't stand a chance without her hair."

"She made her choice and her choice was saving you." April's voice was oddly emotional.

"Me?"

"You're the only one of us they're going to kill on sight. You're the only one who hasn't got anything to fight back with. She told me to keep you safe."

I don't know why those words angered me so much. "Why the *hell* does everyone want to keep me safe?" I screamed. "Why does everyone think I'm such a liability that I can't look after myself?" I saw the girls exchange worried glances out of the corner of my eye and that angered me even more. "I've made it this far, haven't I? Haven't I?" I caught sight of my face in the mirror. I looked terrible. Paler and skinnier than usual. Hair a mess. I very clearly hadn't showered in days and I could see grease and grime smeared all over my skin. And there was fear in my eyes. I hated myself for that.

I didn't want to see myself. I slammed my fist into the mirrored wall, over and over and over again. I didn't feel the shards of glass break. I didn't feel them slice their way into my fingers, covering me in silver slivers. But I knew that's what they were doing, because my hand was wet.

And my reflection was stubbornly still there. Shattered. Fractured. Broken. But still there.

And I was still punching.

Chapter Twenty-Four

Sloths are sometimes known to grab their own arms, instead of tree branches. This can lead to painful falls.

Yeah, no crap. That does sound painful!

Get out of my head, April.

Do you always think of random facts when you're stressed?

It's worked so far. It helped to keep my mind off all the stuff that was going on around me. That, and the blood dripping down my hand from my self-inflicted wound. Why had I done that? That was stupid. And the way everyone had just stared at me, watching me go wild with the mirror, had unnerved me. Nobody had stepped in. Nobody had stopped me. Did they not care if I hurt myself? Obviously not.

We were out of the elevator, creeping though the maze of corridors and hoping we'd be able to sneak out of the complex. It felt like we'd been walking for miles. Blisters were swelling up on my heels and every step made me want to scream.

"Do you hear that?" hissed June, interrupting my unspoken conversation with April. "Voices."

Door 302. It was the nearest and we rushed towards it, while Dad fumbled with his keys. The footsteps were getting closer and closer. Sweat was beading across my forehead. Any minute now, someone was going to come around the corner and then we'd be dead. Suddenly, there was a reassuring click as Dad unlocked the door and we rushed to get inside, closing it behind us as soon as we could. We collectively held our breath. Were the people going to come in here? If so, we were done for. My lungs burned, desperate for air, as the footsteps slowed. Voices sounded outside our door. I wanted January with me. I wanted to reach for her hand and catch her eye. Now, if these people came in here, I wouldn't get to do that again before I died. My heart shuddered. And then they were going past and I let my breath out in a long, relieved swoosh.

But something wasn't quite right. Something felt off. I had the horrible, skin-crawling feeling of eyes on me. The unmistakable feeling that we weren't alone. I turned my head in slow motion, not sure I really wanted to see what else was in the room with us.

When I saw it, I screamed.

Two red eyes were glowing in the dark, staring straight at me.

None of us waited to see who the eyes belonged to. We wrenched the door open and slammed it shut. Something heavy thudded against it and we heard a terrible, low growling. "What the hell was that?" gasped June.

April shook her head. "It wasn't human, I know that for sure."

Realization was dawning on me. "We're so stupid, guys."

They looked at me. "How?"

Panic laced my voice. "If they're willing to play about with human genetics … then what else are they willing to do? Just what kind of creature was that in there?"

"You don't want to know," a voice said, behind us. Ted was standing there, with January beside him. January's hair was ragged, chopped in a rough, edgy bob. It actually suited her. She was the sort of girl who would have suited anything.

I ran to her and held her. "You're still alive!" That's when I noticed the gun Ted was pressing into her back.

"Yeah. For now." January shot a loaded glance at Ted. "Somehow, I don't think we're going to stay that way for very long."

"I agree," Ted said. "I'm very disappointed to see all of you still alive."

"I was bringing them to you, sir," Dad said. "The girls escaped and I found them wandering the corridors."

"With all due respect, Marsh, I call BS." Ted pointed his gun in my dad's direction. "Not to mention the fact that I do have cameras around the place. I saw you break your son out. Should have known better than to trust someone once they're emotionally involved, I suppose."

"What was that creature?" asked my dad, glancing over his shoulder.

"It's just one of the many experiments that go on here," Ted replied. "The main purpose of this lab is to figure out how to create biological weapons to use against other countries. Doesn't matter if they're human or animal or something in between, as long as we can control them."

"And what about us?" demanded June. "Are we just … weapons?"

"We're weapons they can't control," April said, darkly. "And I plan to keep it that way."

"I think me and my gun beg to differ," Ted said, mildly. I'd never hated him more than in that moment. Oh, I'd hated him the moment I walked in his office. I'd hated him when he shot January's mom with no remorse. I'd hated him for getting my dad on his side. But, right then, I hated him for the smug way he was looking at us all. As if we were nothing more than pawns on a chess board, that he could move around as he pleased.

I could feel the adrenaline coursing through my body. It made me feel angry. It made me feel powerful. I had to do what April had asked me to earlier. I had to *end this*. I had to end this man, who thought he had the right to end someone's life as and when he liked. And I knew exactly how to do it.

April. I felt for her mind with mine and her eyes flickered to me.

What?

I need you to open a door for me.

April's eyes widened, just slightly. *Are we running through it?*

Just be ready. Please.

I turned to January. My voice sounded strange to me as I said her name. As if it was coming from somewhere very far away.

She turned to look at me. Why is it the right words are never there when you need them? I had so much I needed to say, and I could feel time slipping through my fingers. "You're my best friend," I said. "I'll always love you."

And I wrenched on the handle of door 302. *Now, April!* I screamed in my head.

April reacted instantly, slamming her thumb on the keypad and staring at the scanner. I pictured her brainwaves, waving and wiggling in the air, sending false signals to the machines. I pictured my plan not working. I pictured Ted shooting me as I tugged on the door handle.

But before Ted could react, before he could stop me, I felt the click of the locks release and the door flew open in my hands.

The creature had been pressed against the door and almost fell out into the corridor. Red eyes, shaggy fur, and more teeth than a mouthwash commercial. If I had to guess, I'd say it was part wolf, but the animal's genus was the last thing on my mind right then.

Ted's eyes widened in horror. "You fool," he

snapped, turning his gun towards the creature. "Do you have any idea how dangerous it is?"

I didn't plan on sticking around to find out. I caught hold of April and January and I screamed: "Run!"

And then we were running, flying through the corridors, blindly following my dad and hoping he knew the right way to go (although how could he? How could any of us?). I glanced over my shoulder to see the enormous wolf-thing advancing on Ted, and then I turned a corner and didn't look back. Gunshots sounded in the distance along with a terrible howling. I just hoped the howling was from Ted and not the creature. With any luck it had killed him.

"April, open every door you can!" screamed June.

April did her best, picking random doors as she ran past—and the creatures of your worst nightmares flooded out.

Have you ever wanted to see a giant rat with skin like a lizard? No? Me neither, but it lumbered out of one of the rooms. Experiment after experiment, freak after freak, mutant after mutant… You get the idea.

A swarm of butterflies poured out of one room. Glow-in-the-dark butterflies. "Aw, so cute!" cooed April, as one landed on her finger. "Ow, damn! It bit me!"

Sirens screamed. "Red alert," boomed the speakers. "Lockdown initiated."

"Run! If the building's locked down, we can't escape!" cried Dad.

We were all running again, not stopping to open any more doors. My heart was aching inside my chest, ready to burst with effort. Partition doors were sliding downwards from the ceiling, cutting off the corridors in increments.

"We need to hurry!" screamed June. "We can't let ourselves be trapped!"

The slamming sound of metal against floor echoed behind us as we just managed to keep a few steps ahead of the doors.

Daylight. Beautiful, magical, grey daylight. I could see it through two swing doors. Framed by two burly guards with guns.

"Stop right there!"

We didn't. We kept running. The guards raised their weapons and then saw the chaos behind us. Screams were echoing behind us, along with unearthly howls and grunts from whatever those bizarre animals were. The guards looked at each other and fled. We followed, slamming the doors behind us.

Chapter Twenty-Five

Bees can live inside your eyes and feed on your sweat.

That fact used to freak me out. But, after you've been chased by mad scientists, seen dozens of weird genetically modified creatures, and have three friends with superpowers, then your freak-out tolerance gets a lot higher.

My dad sprinted over to a battered old SUV, the only vehicle in the enormous compound. "The keys are inside. Let's go." We piled in. My dad got in the driver's seat and the engine roared into life.

"Seatbelts, children!" trilled April. She was being brave, but I could see the way she kept cradling her injured arm and her face was as white as a sheet.

Dad slammed his foot on the accelerator and we lurched away in what was presumably going to be my second car chase of the week. We flew through barriers. ("Badass," commented June.)

Was I the only one noticing the path was becoming more overgrown? It hadn't been like that on the way in, had it? Or maybe I just hadn't noticed?

No. The road had suddenly tapered out and we were driving on grass.

"Dad, please tell me this is a shortcut?" I asked.

"I must have taken a wrong turn." He cursed and punched the steering wheel.

"A wrong turn? You're supposed to be the one who knows where we're going!" I screamed.

"In case you didn't notice, they didn't exactly have an exit sign!" he yelled back, stopping the car.

"What do we do?" asked January, in a voice so quiet I barely heard her. "By now, they're bound to have got themselves together. They might be on our tails as we speak."

"Where exactly are we?" I got out of the SUV and everyone followed me. The wind whipped tears into my eyes. We were standing on top of a cliff, looking down at the angry sea.

"Um, guys… Do you hear that?" June's head was tilted to one side. I heard it then. The sound of a helicopter approaching in the distance.

"Quick, make for the trees!" Dad yelled.

"Too late." Another SUV was zooming towards us. Inside, I recognized Ted and two of his cronies.

My mind was racing. In my head, I could see images of my friends—gunned down by the men in the helicopters. Shot in cold blood by Ted and his men. Driven over the cliff. In every possible outcome, we all died.

Life was an hourglass. And our time had just run out.

I looked at my dad and held out my hand. With a puzzled look on his face, he took it and shook it. "Keep the girls safe," I said.

"Why?" he wanted to know.

I didn't answer and turned to January, held her face in my hands and kissed her. "I love you." Funny how it was so easy then, when it really was the end of everything, to say what I wanted to say. Funny how the words just slipped off my tongue when I knew they would be the last words I'd ever say to her.

April was standing in front of me and I touched her shoulder. She turned. I kissed her cheek. "I owe you."

She smiled. "I know."

I laughed. "Never change, April." *Now start running, take the others with you, and keep them safe.*

She must have heard my thoughts, because she grabbed her sisters' hands and pulled them after her. She never asked any questions. Maybe she already knew what my answer would be.

I leapt into the SUV's driving seat and started the engine up. Ted and his men were already driving after the girls.

"What are you doing?" demanded Dad.

"Keep the girls safe!" I repeated. And then I hit the accelerator and roared off, heading straight for the other SUV. Gunshots sprayed after me. I wasn't sure if they was from the helicopter or Ted and I really didn't care. I was between them and the girls, and that's all that mattered. The helicopter couldn't touch them if they were in the woods and I saw with relief that April had managed to get them all there. April, who had taken such a battering. April, who might be dying. Couldn't think about that right now.

No matter which way Ted tried to steer his SUV, I intercepted. I was leading him where I wanted him to, and he never even knew it. I was guiding him into the exact position. My heart was hammering inside my chest. I could feel adrenaline pulsing its way through my body. It made me feel powerful.

Ted and his men were exactly where I wanted them to be, between me and the cliff. Ted leaned out the window. "Stop. This doesn't end well for any of us if you keep doing this."

"It was never going to end well after you decided to kidnap twelve babies!" I screamed at him. That would have been the moment for a speech. If I was the hero in this story, maybe I could have thought of one. But all I could think of was the truth. "Don't you get it? There is no happy ending here."

I slammed my foot against the pedal and the SUV shot forward, ramming straight into Ted's. He and I were almost face to face, peering at each other through the cracked windscreen. He was mouthing "No, stop!" at me over and over. My foot was still on the accelerator, although my leg was bouncing with nerves and adrenaline. My SUV was creeping forward, inch by inch, slipping and sliding on the muddy ground, but still going forward.

Ted was scrabbling at the door, desperately trying to get out. I was losing time. I slammed the SUV into a different gear and hit the accelerator again with all my might.

The last thing I saw before I drove over the cliff was Ted and his two men falling down before me.

Chapter Twenty-Six

A human head remains conscious for around 20 seconds after being decapitated.

And, because I'm feeling generous, here's a bonus fact for you.

Around half the population believes in some form of ghost or spirit.

I never used to be one of them, though.

They say when you're unconscious that everything goes black.

It doesn't. At least, it didn't for me.

Everything was blinding white—like heaven, like angels, like sunshine. I couldn't tell if I was drowning or floating, sinking or flying. In some respects, it's all the same.

Was there pain, or was there nothing at all? Was I conscious or was I dreaming? Maybe I was dreaming.

In my dreams, Sam had saved us all. He'd called, not the police, but the newspapers. He'd made them listen to our crazy story. He'd got our names and our faces plastered across the front pages of every newspaper. He'd pointed the finger at the laboratory, at the scientists, and at the organization that was behind it all. He was giving exclusive interviews—telling the whole story. Making sure the girls were safe. They became famous, doing interviews on talk shows, demonstrating how their powers worked for the whole world to see. It was nice to see them looking happy. It was nice to see January not looking over her shoulder or April not picking nervously at the skin around her thumbs.

Ted and his two men died after I knocked them over the cliff. Everyone said it was self-defense on my part. I suppose it was, but I'd wanted to hurt them. I'd wanted to hurt them like they'd hurt so many. I told you I wasn't the hero in this story. Heroes don't kill people, do they? Maybe I'd see them all in hell. I'd find out soon enough. The rest of the people who worked in that lab either ran or hid or denied all knowledge that there was anything shady going on.

Ginger was given a proper funeral—and not the kind where a preacher who doesn't know you says nice things about you. The best kind, the kind where we all shared a memory we had about Ginger.

I was there, standing off to the side. It didn't feel real. *I* didn't feel real.

Somehow, nobody asked me for my memory. But I knew what I would have said if they had. My memory would have been the time we were all eleven and we went fishing by the river. I cut my finger on a fish hook and it hurt so badly I nearly cried. But I would have bled to death before I admitted in front of Sam and James that I was hurt. Ginger knew that. She saw me, she saw the blood leaking through my skin, and she stood up and said she was bored and could I take her home.

She never said a word all the way home, but she walked me to my house and told me to bandage my finger. I was too shy and too embarrassed to thank her.

Nobody wore black. Somehow, we all knew Ginger wouldn't have wanted that.

My dad was there. And his arm was around my mother. I couldn't remember the last time I'd seen them stand so close. Not without yelling at each other.

James cried for the whole funeral. I'd never seen him cry before.

And Sam. Sam was almost inconsolable. He hadn't even been that close to Ginger.

Even January, April, and June, who hardly knew Ginger, were crying. They were wearing their brightest colors and looked like rainbow girls.

I wasn't standing with them, and I didn't know why. Every time I tried to move, my legs felt like they were stuck in molasses. I could only watch them, see their heads bowed in respect and sorrow as they looked down at the grave.

January's hair was black, framing her pale, thin face. She looked like she hadn't slept in weeks. Dark shadows lurked under her eyes and her bottom lip kept wobbling. I wanted to go over and comfort her, but I was frozen.

April, with her lust for life and her invasive mind powers and her magic smile. The way she bailed my ass out, the way she called me out when I was burying my head in the sand. I needed her. I wondered if she needed me. I could see her face twist in pain every so often, and she kept holding her arm where she had been shot, but she was alive. Gloriously, ridiculously, delightfully alive.

And June. Her arms folded across her chest, wearing a long black coat. Her eyes were red. She hadn't even met Ginger.

Why was everyone so sad?

Why did they seem so far away from me?

Ginger's parents made a tearful speech and then James stood up to say something. "She was more than just my girlfriend. She was my best friend. She didn't deserve what happened to her. Right now, she should be having the time of her life." His voice cracked. "My only consolation is that the people who did this to her got what they deserved. Thanks to Leon."

"Sam is going to say a few words," my dad said, quietly. His voice sounded like it was underwater.

Sam swiped at his eyes and walked into the middle of the group, by the mound of dirt. "Friendship is precious," he gulped. His voice sounded thick with tears. "And I know if…" He swallowed hard and fought to keep himself together, shoving his glasses up the bridge of his nose. "I know if they were looking down on us right now, they'd be laughing at the state we're in. They'd be saying things like 'Cheer up.' They'd be trying to make us feel better." Sam took a deep breath and tugged at his left earlobe, the way he always did when he was nervous. "The truth is, I knew Leon better than anyone else in the world. We were best friends. For life. And I saw the way he looked at January when she walked into school. He knew, right then, that he was in trouble."

January raised her eyes to Sam and she looked like she was trying to laugh but was crying instead. I could see her shoulders shaking.

"So I know that Leon would have no regrets," continued Sam. "If he had to do it all over again, he would. He was that kind of guy. He'd do anything to save the people he cared about." Sam lost control of his voice and squeaked on the last word. I wanted to tease him about it. I wanted to ask him why he was giving a speech about me when it was Ginger's funeral. Sam's shoulders were heaving now and his eyes were shiny. "I'm going to miss him," was all he choked out before he went to stand with January.

I was feeling cold now, but cold from the inside. Something was scratching at the back of my mind, a question I had to ask but didn't want answered.

My legs moved now, almost of their own accord. I was floating, definitely floating, over to them. I was almost above them, but my feet felt like they were on the ground. That definitely wasn't normal. Maybe I had a concussion. I guess that was to be expected after falling over a cliff.

No, this wasn't a concussion. I'd had a concussion when I fell off a swing four years ago. Concussion was pain and feeling sick and a little dizzy. This was …

almost peaceful. Almost like my body and mind were separated, but still connected. I couldn't move, I could only think. Something was wrong. I liked it, but I didn't like it.

The question was forming itself in my brain and I knew my time was running out. I had to ask it now, no matter how much the answer hurt.

Why were the girls crying so hard for someone they hardly knew?

And I knew then what I'd known all along.

I didn't want to look, but my eyes drifted down of their own accord.

There were two coffins being lowered into the ground.

And one of them was mine.

The End

ROZ MACLAREN

Evernight Teen ®

www.evernightteen.com